哈福

哈福

哈福

＼ 出國旅遊，看這本就夠了 ／

世界最簡單
自助旅行英語

一生必遊的100個世界熱門景點，簡單英語就行了！
迅速教會你敢講、敢說，一個人全世界旅遊也不怕！

May I help you?
你需要什麼嗎？

I'm just looking.
我只是看看。

附QR碼線上音檔
行動學習 即刷即聽

施孝昌 ◎著

哈福

出國旅遊， 看這本就夠了

迅速教會你敢講、敢說，
一個人全世界旅遊也不怕！

出國觀光，最怕聽不懂，說不出。

很多朋友都有過這種經驗：面對美食不知如何點餐，看到喜愛的東西不會開口洽購，車來車往，不知該坐哪一線；住在旅館，想叫客房服務不知從何說起…，一趟比手劃腳下來，已是人仰馬翻，遊興盡失。

繞著地球跑，已是現代人的生活目標之一；想要看盡世間奇景，遍嚐各地美味，結交各國朋友，清晰流利的英語，就是您暢遊天下的一大保證。

針對此點，我們特地為愛好觀光旅行的朋友，設計簡單易學的英語好書，我們的特色是：

簡單好學：每個單字片語在中學時都已學過，簡單易懂，絕無難字，可以現學現用，省卻您寶貴的時間和精力。

活潑實用：〈實況會話〉生動活潑，切合實際生活需要，純正美語，絕不讓您學到累贅又不實用的洋涇濱英語。

資料豐富：每個CHAPTER的〈旅遊錦囊〉提醒您旅途中必須注意的細節及重要事項，保障您的權益，省卻不必要的麻煩糾紛。

解釋最詳：〈句型分析〉詳細解釋各句型的適用情形，避免語意不清；〈句型練習〉則針對主題基本例句加以變化，更加豐富您使用的詞彙語句。

　　海外旅遊「死忠」跟著導遊，任人刀俎宰割的時代已經過去。講究獨立自主的新人類，不僅要玩得安全，玩出品質，行程個性化及自由化更是最新的追求目標。明確清楚的英語表達能力，加上良好的行程規劃，就是您成功出擊的利器。

　　別忘了要多聽外師的專業錄音，但語調、發音需要有人示範才學得好，所以跟著外師學習，效果才是最好的！輕輕鬆鬆學會觀光英語，讓您說出自信，得意上路，一書在手，不再羨慕別人，自己也可以做個環遊世界的超級玩家。

　　因應時代與科技進步，本書以「附免費QR碼線上音檔」，全新呈現給讀者，行動學習，即刷即聽，英語實力進步更神速。

Vacation Trip

Travel By Air

Chapter 3

Renting a Car

Chapter 4

At Hotel

Chapter 5

Food and Drink

Chapter 6

In the Department Store

Chapter 7

In the Supermarket

Chapter 8

Around Town

Chapter 9

Making Phone Calls

At the Gas Station

Transportation

心情筆記

Vacation Trip

旅行計劃開始

好不容易有個假期，
到美國去散心吧，
終於連行程都訂好了，
可以昭告天下。
這樣的消息
要如何正確地宣佈呢？

實況會話　宣告旅行計畫

旅　客	I'm going to the United States next week. 我下星期要去美國。
朋　友	Is that right?　Is it a business trip? 是嗎？是商務旅行嗎？
旅　客	No, I am going to visit some friends in California and New York. 不是，我要去加州和紐約拜訪一些朋友。
朋　友	That's great. I hope you have a good time in America. 那好棒，祝你在美國玩得愉快。
	By the way, if you need a ride to the airport. I'll be happy to take you. 還有，如果你需要有人載你去機場，我很樂意載你。
旅　客	Oh, thanks. That's very nice of you. 噢，謝謝，你真好。
	But, I'm going to take the taxi to the airport. 但，我想搭計程車去機場。
朋　友	Will anyone pick you up at the Los Angeles airport? 在洛杉磯機場有人會來接你嗎？
旅　客	No, I will rent a car at the airport. 沒有，我會在機場租車。

 句型分析

→ 到國外去旅行，想昭告天下，就用I'm going to＋地名，就可以了。

→ 任何人跟你講一件事，你都可以用Is that right?或That's great.來回答，表示你的興趣。

→ 聽到別人有任何計劃，你若願意幫忙的話，可以用If you need～, let me know.

→ 謝謝別人提議的好意，要說That's very nice of you.若要用It's very nice of you.句子要繼續說完，It 指那件事。例如：It's very nice of you to give me a ride. It 指to give me a ride這件事不可以只說It's very nice of you.

 句型練習

與車子接送有關的句型

❖ If you need somebody to help you, let me know.

如果你需要有人幫你，讓我知道。

❖ If you need a ride, I'll be happy to take you.

如果你需要有人載，我很樂意載你。

❖ Could you give me a ride home?

你可以載我回家嗎？

❖ Could you give me a ride to the airport?

你可以載我到去機場嗎？

❖ Could you pick me up at the airport?

你可以到機場接我嗎？

❖ Will anyone pick you up at the airport?

有人會去機場接你嗎？

❖ I can't give you a ride. I need to go to the airport to pick up my friend.

我不能載你，我要去機場接我的朋友。

vacation trip [ve'keʃən trɪp] 度假	business trip ['bɪzɪnɪs trɪp] 商務旅行	visit ['vɪzɪt] 拜訪
airport ['ɛrport] 機場	shuttle ['ʃʌtl̩] 在機場和市區來回行駛的車子	ride [raɪd] （用車子）載
taxi 計程車		

Chapter 2

Travel By Air
機場會話

到海外旅行，搭飛機是最方便的交通工具。搭飛機旅行，從到機場報到，以及在飛機上，有那些需注意的英語句型呢？

Unit 1

Check-in
到機場報到

◆ 對話一：報到

服務員	Good afternoon. 午安。
	Your ticket and passport, please. 請給我看你的機票和護照。
旅 客	Here you are. 在這兒。
服務員	Thank you. 謝謝你。
	Would you put your baggage here？ 請把你的行李放這裡？
	I'll check it through. 我要登記。
旅 客	Sure. 好的。

服務員	There will be a 20-minute delay, so your flight will be boarding in about an hour.
	飛機誤點二十分，所以你的班機會在一小時後登機。

◆ 對話二：把行李交給航空公司

服務員	Please set your baggage upright here.
	請把你的行李擺直放在這裏。
	I'll have to weigh it.
	我要秤多重。

（過磅後……）

	The baggage is overweight, sir.
	先生，你的行李超重。
	You have to pay $65.00.
	你要付六十五美元。
旅　客	Can I charge it on credit cards?
	我可以用信用卡嗎？
服務員	Yes. We accept major credit cards.
	可以，我們收主要的信用卡。

◆ 對話三：通過安全門

服務員	Put all your carry-on bags on the belt, sir.
	把你隨身攜帶的袋子放在輸送帶上。

旅　客	The camera, too? 照相機也要嗎？
服務員	Yes, please. It won't hurt your film. 是的，不會損壞底片的。
	Now, step through here. 現在，從這裏走過去。

◆ 對話四：安全門的警鈴響了

服務員	Are you wearing any metal? 你戴任何金屬品嗎？
旅　客	I don't know. 我不知道。
	Maybe it's the belt. 可能是這條皮帶。
服務員	Take it off and put it on the box here. 脫下來，放在這個盒子上。
	And walk through again. 再重走一次。
	That's fine. Here's your belt. 沒問題了，你的皮帶拿回去。
旅　客	Thank you. 謝謝你。

◆ 對話五：道別上飛機

Announcement: "Flight 801 to Taipei is now boarding at Gate 3." 廣播：往台北801次班機現在在3號門登機。

旅　客	That's my flight. 那是我的班機。	
	I've got to go. Bye. 我要走了，再見。	
送　行	Bye. Have a nice flight. 再見，祝你旅途愉快。	
	Give me a call when you get there. 到了之後，打個電話給我。	

句型分析

→　要求對方做某事，可以直接用命令句，Put your bags on the belt.但也可以說得委婉些，用Would you～？或 Would you please～？的句型。後者表面上是「你是否可以做某事？」像疑問句，但實際上只是較客套的請對方做某事。在這裡用Would you put your bags on the belt?與Put your bags on the belt.意思是一樣的。

到機場報到

❖ Your ticket and passport, please.

請讓我看你的機票和護照。

❖ Would you like a window seat or an aisle seat?

你要坐靠窗還是靠走道的位子?

❖ Smoking or non-smoking?

吸煙區還是非吸煙區?

❖ Here are your baggage claim checks.

這是你的行李提取單。

❖ Your flight will be boarding in 20 minutes.

你的班機在二十分鐘後登機。

❖ Have a nice flight.

祝你飛行愉快。

通過安全門

❖ Put all your carry-on bags on the belt.

把你隨身攜帶的袋子放在輸送帶上。

❖ Put the keys on the box over here.

把鑰匙放在這個盒子裏。

❖ Are you wearing any metal?

你戴金屬品嗎？

❖ Step through here.

從這裡走過去。

重要單字

airline ['ɛrlaɪn]	航空公司
airport ['ɛrport]	機場
air fare [ɛr fɛr]	飛機票價
flight [flaɪt]	班機
freight [fret]	貨物；航空運輸
route [raʊt]	路線
delay [dɪ'le]	誤點
timetable ['taɪmtebḷ]	時刻
first class [fɜst klæs]	頭等艙
economy class [ɪ'kɑnəmɪ klæs]	經濟艙
check-in ['tʃɛk ɪn]	報到
board [bord]	登機
boarding pass ['bordɪŋ pæs]	登機卡
gate [get]	登機門
standby ['stændbaɪ]	候補
baggage ['bægɪdʒ]	行李
carry-on baggage ['kærɪ ɑn 'bægɪdʒ]	隨身行李
overweight ['ovɚwet]	超重
baggage claim ticket ['bægɪdʒ klem 'tɪkɪt]	行李提取單
baggage claim area ['bægɪdʒ klem 'ɛrɪə]	行李提取區

In the Plane
在飛機上

◆ 對話一：向空中小姐要東西

旅　客	Could you bring me a blanket, please? 可否請你拿條毯子給我？
空　姐	Sure, I'll get one for you later. 好的，我待會兒拿一條給你。

◆ 對話二：空中小姐提供飲料

空　姐	Anything to drink? 你要喝什麼嗎？
旅　客	Yes, give me white wine. 好的，請給我白酒。
空　姐	Do you want ice with it? 你要加冰嗎？
旅　客	No, thank you. 不用，謝謝你。

◆ 對話三：提供餐飲

空　姐	Excuse me, do you want beef or chicken meal for lunch? 對不起，你要牛肉餐還是雞肉餐？
旅　客	Chicken, please. 我要雞肉餐。
空　姐	What do you want to drink? 你要喝什麼？
旅　客	Orange juice, please. 柳橙汁。

 句型分析

→ 請別人拿東西給你，用Could you bring me～?

→ 問對方有什麼種類的，用What kind of～do you have?
或What kind of～would you serve?

 句型練習

提供飲料

❖ Anything to drink?

要喝什麼嗎？

❖ What would you like to drink?

你要喝什麼？

❖ What do you want to drink?

你要喝什麼？

要東西

❖ Could you bring me some magazines?

你可否拿一些雜誌給我？

❖ What kind of drinks do you have?

你有什麼飲料？

❖ What kind of wine would you serve?

你有什麼酒？

blanket ['blæŋkɪt]	毯子
beef [bif]	牛肉
meal [mil]	（三）餐

◆ 對話一：問如何轉機

旅客 1	I'm a transit passenger. 我是一個過境旅客。
	What am I going to do now? 我現在該做什麼？
服務員	Check in at the transfer counter over there. 在那邊那個過境櫃台報到。
	And get your boarding pass for New York. 拿你到紐約的登機卡。
	Then go directly to the transit lounge and wait for your flight to board. 然後直接到過境休息室去，等你的班機。

◆ 對話二：在過境櫃台

| 地　勤 | May I help you?
有什麼事嗎？ |

旅　客	I'm on my way to New York. 我要去紐約。
	Is this the interline transfer counter? 這裏是過境櫃台嗎？
地　勤	Yes. May I see your ticket? 是的，請給我看你的機票。

（ 看完後…… ）

Here you go. The boarding pass. Flight 402 will be boarding at Gate 3 in two hours.
在這兒。你的登機卡，402號班機會在二小時後在三號門登機。

句型分析

→ 過境櫃台，英文可以説transfer counter，或interline transfer counter。

→ 問別人該如何轉機，可以説I'm a transits passenger. What am I going to do now?或是How do I transfer to 某地？

過境轉機

❖ I'm a transit passenger.
我是個過境旅客。

❖ How do I transfer to New York?
我要如何轉機到紐約？

❖ I'm on my way to Chicago.
我要前往芝加哥。

❖ Is this the interline transfer counter?
這裡是過境櫃台嗎？

❖ Is this the transfer counter?
這裡是過境櫃台嗎？

❖ Which gate am I supposed to board at?
我應該在那個登機門登機？

transit ['trænzɪt]	過境
transit passenger ['trænzɪt 'pæsɪndʒɚ]	過境旅客
transfer counter ['trænsfɚ 'kaʊntɚ]	過境櫃台
interline transfer counter ['ɪntɚlaɪn]	過境櫃台
transit lounge ['trænzɪt laʊndʒ]	轉機休息室
rest room ['rɛstrum]	廁所

Unit 4

Customs

海關

◆ 對話一：海關人員問話

關　員	May I see your passport, please? 請給我看你的護照，好嗎？
旅　客	Sure, here you are. 好的，在這兒。
關　員	What's the purpose of your trip? 你這次旅行的目的是什麼？
旅　客	I am here to visit my friends. 我來此訪友。
關　員	How long are you going to stay in the States? 你要在美國停留多久？
旅　客	I'm going to stay for three weeks. 我要停留三個星期。

◆ 對話二：通關

關 員	Do you have anything to declare? 你有什麼東西要申報嗎？
旅 客	I don't think so. 應該沒有。
	I have some souvenirs as gifts for my friends, and a used camcorder for my personal use. 我有一些紀念品是要給朋友的禮物，還有一個舊的攝錄影機是我自用的

句型分析

→ 問對方要求，用May I～?的句型是客氣的說法，例如，海關人員說May I see your passport?是表示要看你的護照，並不是真的在徵求你的同意。他可以直接了當說，Passport, please.同樣是表示要看你的護照。

句型練習

海關問話

❖ What's the purpose of your trip?

你此次旅遊的目的是什麼？

❖ I am here on vacation.

我來度假。

❖ I am here on business.

我來做生意。

❖ I am here to visit my friends.

我來訪友。

❖ I am here for a conference.

我來開會。

❖ I am here as a student.

我來留學。

通關

❖ Do you have anything to declare?

你有沒有什麼東西要申報？

❖ I have a camcorder for personal use.

我有一個自用的攝錄影機。

❖ I bought some souvenirs as gifts for my friends.

我買了一些紀念品給朋友當禮物。

❖ I have some wines that I bought at the duty-free shop.

我有幾瓶在免稅商店買的酒。

customs [ˈkʌstəmz]	海關
customs officer	海關人員
customs declaration [ˈkʌstəmz dɛkləˈreʃən]	報關
declare [dɪˈklɛr]	申報
declaration form	申報單
duty-free shop	免稅商店
duty-free merchandise [ˌdjutɪ fri ˈmɝtʃəndaɪz]	免稅商品
visa [ˈvizə]	簽證

旅 遊 錦 囊

　　到外國，你可以在機場租車，這樣就可以省掉請別人接機的麻煩。有關租車的會話句型，在 chapter 3（第三章）有詳細說明。在國外，有些機場有市區公車到市區，或是有些旅館的shuttle往返於機場和該旅館之間。在出發旅行之前，最好先問清楚。因為並不是每個機場都有電影上所演出的一長排的計程車在機場外候客，也沒有隨叫隨到的方便，所以一切要靠自己那一口靈光的英語了。

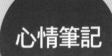

Chapter 3

Renting a Car
租車

到了機場，想要租車，
記得把以下句型背熟，
可使租車情況順利，
又不致被敲詐。

◆ 對話一：租車

旅　客	How much is it to rent an economy car? 租一輛小型車要多少錢？
服務員	$35.00 a day or $175.00 a week. 一天35美元，一星期是175元。
旅　客	O.K. I'll take it right now, if possible. 好的，如果可以的話，我現在就要租車。
服務員	Do you have any major credit cards? 你有沒有信用卡？
旅　客	Yes, I have master card. 有的，我有萬士達卡。
服務員	Can I see your driver's license? 請給我看你的駕駛執照？
旅　客	Sure, here you are. My international driver's license. 好的，在這兒，我的國際駕駛執照。
服務員	Good. Fill out this form and sign your name at the bottom. 好，把這張表填好，在底下簽名。

◆ 對話二：在別州還車

| 旅　客 | Can I leave the car in another state?
我可以在別州還車嗎？ |

服務員	Yes, but there is surcharge if you return the car at another branch. 可以，但是你如果在別的分行還車的話，我們要額外收費。
旅　客	How much would you charge? 要收多少錢？
服務員	Let me check. 我查查看。

◆ 對話三：還車

旅　客	I am here to return the car I rented. 我來還我租的車子。
	I parked it out there. And here are the keys. 我把車子停在外面，鑰匙在這裡。
服務員	Is the gas full? 加滿油了嗎？
旅　客	Yes, I just filled it up. 是，我剛加滿。
服務員	O.K. The total is $50.10. 好的，總共50元10分。
旅　客	Here. Fifty dollars and ten cents. 在這兒，50元10分。
服務員	Thank you. Have a nice day. 謝謝，祝你一天都愉快。

旅　客	Thank you. You too.
	謝謝，你也一樣。

→ 美國人分手前，常會説句，Have a nice day.聽到這句話，你就説Thank you. You too.

→ 問租車多少錢，也可以用What's the rate for a car?

→ 想要租車，先要把價錢打聽清楚。問價錢，最簡單的句型是，How much is某某東西？但此處要租車（rent a car）是動詞，所以在某某東西的位置上用it後面才用不定詞to rent a car,句型就變成How much is it to＋動詞？

→ 當價錢談妥時，你就要租車了，這裡的「要」不可用want，需用I'll take it，用take來表示對方所描述的東西，你還算滿意，所以你要它。

租車

❖ Do you have any mid-size car available?
你有沒有中型車出租？

❖ Do you have a four-door sedan for tomorrow?
你有沒有四門轎車明天可以租給我？

❖ Do you have a van for three days, starting next Monday.

你有沒有小巴士，我可以從下星期一起租三天。

❖ I'd like to rent an economy-size car.

我要租輛小型車。

❖ I'd like to rent a station wagon for the weekend.

我這個週末要租輛旅行車。

❖ I'd like to rent a van for a week, starting tomorrow.

我想租一輛小巴士，從明天起租一個星期。

問租車行情（請注意聽MP3，有關錢的英語的正確說法。）

❖ How much is it to rent a mid-size car?

租一輛中型車要多少錢？

❖ How much does it cost to rent a small car?

租輛小車要多少錢？

❖ If I wanted to rent a van, how much would it be?

如果我要租一輛旅行車，要多少錢？

❖ What's the rate for a station wagon?

租一部旅行車，要多少錢？

❖ What's the daily rate for an economy car?

租一部小型車，每天要多少錢？

❖ What's the weekly rate for a mid-size car?

租一部中型車，每週多少錢？

❖ What's the weekend rate for a van?

租一部小巴士，週末要多少錢？

租車行情（請注意聽MP3，有關錢的英語的正確說法。）

❖ $25.00 a day or $130.00 a week, unlimited mileage.

一天25元，一星期是130元，不限里程數。

❖ It would be $ 45.00 a day or $280.00 a week.

一天45元，一星期是280元。

在別州還車

❖ Can I leave the car at another agency?

我可以在別的車行還車嗎？

❖ Do I have to return the car here?

我一定要在這裡還車嗎？

❖ Can I leave the car in another state?

我可以在別州還車嗎？

租車

❖ I'd like one for the weekend.

我這個週末要一輛車。

❖ I'll take it right now, if possible.

如果可以，我現在就要。

❖ I'd like to reserve one for next Monday.

我要預定一輛車，下星期一要。

❖ I'll need one for a week, starting tomorrow.

我從明天起要租一星期。

看證件

❖ Do you have any major credit cards?

你有信用卡嗎？

❖ May I see your driver's license?

我可以看你的駕駛執照嗎？

還車

❖ I'm returning the car. Here are the keys.

我來還車。鑰匙在這兒。

❖ I am here to return the car. I parked it out there.

我來還車，我把車停在外面。

small car [smɔl kɑr]	小型汽車
economy car [ɪˈkɑnəmɪ]	經濟型汽車；小型車
mid-size car [mɪd saɪz]	中型汽車
four-door sedan [ˈdæn]	四門轎車
luxury car [ˈlʌkʃərɪ]	豪華車
big car	大車
van [væn]	小巴士
station wagon [ˈsteʃən ˈwægən]	旅行車
sports car [spɔrts kɑr]	跑車
rent-a-car office	租車公司
rent [rɛnt]	租
return	退還
major credit card [ˌmedʒɚ krɛdɪt ˈkɑrd]	主要的信用卡
unlimited mileage [ʌnˈlɪmɪtɪd ˈmaɪlɪdʒ]	不限里程
driver's license [ˈdraɪvɚz ˈlaɪsəns]	駕駛執照

旅遊錦囊

轉機並不是那麼簡單的一件事，有時候，你需要走很遠去轉機，你若對那個機場不熟的話，可以向你搭乘的航空公司要求派個人帶你到你所要轉的下一班登機門去。千萬別一個人亂走迷了路，還可能接不上飛機，那麻煩可更大了。

Chapter 4

At Hotel

住旅館

到了美國，想住旅館，
進了旅館門，
該如何向櫃台的職員
要房間住呢？
請記住以下句型。

◆ 對話一：有雙人房嗎？

旅　客	Do you have a double room? 你們有雙人房嗎？
服務員	Yes, we have a nice one. 有的，我們有間很好的雙人房。
旅　客	How much would it be? 要多少錢？
服務員	$60.00, plus tax. 60美元，稅外加。
旅　客	Fine. Could you show it to me, please? 好的，可以讓我看看嗎？
服務員	Sure, the bellboy will show you the way. 好的，服務生會帶路。

◆ 對話二：全客滿了

旅　客	Do you have any single rooms available? 你們有單人房嗎？
服務員	I'm sorry, sir, but we're all booked up for the weekend. 對不起，先生，但是這個週末我們全客滿了。
旅　客	Oh, that's too bad. Thank you. 噢，那真是太糟了，謝謝你。

◆ 對話三：預訂了房間

旅　客	Hi, I've got a reservation for a double room. My name is John Lee. 嗨，我預訂了一間雙人房，名字叫李約翰。
服務員	Here we are. Room 206. 是的，有登記是206號房。
	Please fill out the registration form. 請填，這張登記表。
旅　客	Sure. 好的。
服務員	Here are the keys. 鑰匙在這兒。
旅　客	Thank you. 謝謝你。

◆ 對話四：服務生帶路

服務員	Over here, please. 往這兒走。
旅　客	Is Room Service available twenty-four hours? 24小時都有客房服務嗎？
服務員	Yes. Anything I can get for you? 是的，你需要我幫你送什麼東西來嗎？

旅　客	No, thanks. 沒有，謝謝你。
服務員	Well, if you need anything, just call the bell captain. The number's on the phone. 如果你需要什麼東西，打電話給服務生領班，號碼就在電話上。

◆ 對話五：冷氣壞了

旅　客	Excuse me. There's something you could help me with. 對不起，我需要你幫我一點忙。
服務員	What's the problem? 有什麼問題嗎？
旅　客	The air conditioning doesn't work in my room. 我房裏的冷氣機壞了。
服務員	Oh, I'm sorry. I'll have someone check it right away. 對不起，我馬上派人去看看。
旅　客	Thank you. 謝謝。

句型分析

→ 到了旅館，要房間住，你可以很簡單地問，Do you have a～?後面接你所要的房間，例如你要單人房，就說single room，要雙人房就說double room，要套房就說Suite.

→ 你問多少錢時，對方如果說"$60.00,plus tax."就表示六十元，不包括稅，你付賬時還要另外加稅一起付。如果說"$60.00 including tax."或"$60.00 tax included."就表示，他所報的價錢已包括稅，所以付賬時只要付六十元就行。

句型練習

登記住宿

❖ Hi, we're the Wangs. We're checking in.

嗨！我們姓王，我們要登記住宿。

❖ Hi, I've got a reservation for a double room. My name is Mary Lin.

嗨！我預訂了一間雙人房，我名字叫林瑪麗。

❖ Do you have any double rooms available?

你有雙人房嗎？

❖ Do you have a double room?

你有雙人房嗎？

請客房服務

服務員	Room Service. May I help you? 這裡客房服務處，有什麼事嗎？
旅　客	I'd like to order a bacon and egg breakfast, and an orange juice, please. 我想要點一份培根蛋當早餐，還要一杯柳橙汁。

洗衣服務

服務員	Laundry service. May I help you? 這裡是洗衣服務處，有什麼事嗎？
旅　客	I would like to have my suit pressed, please. 我的套裝需要熨一熨。

定時起床服務

服務員	Wake-up service. May I help you? 叫醒人的服務處，有什麼事嗎？
旅　客	Would you please call me at 7:00 tomorrow morning? 你可以在明早七點叫醒我嗎？

重要單字

single room [ˈʃɪŋgl̩ rum]	單人房
double room [ˈdʌbl̩]	雙人房
suite [swit]	套房
available [əˈveləbl̩]	有效的；有空的
front desk [frʌnt dɛsk]	櫃台
problem [ˈprɑbləm]	問題
room service	客房服務
laundry service [ˈlɔndrɪ ˈsɝvɪs]	洗衣服務
wake-up service	叫醒人服務
tip	小費
bellboy	服務生
bell captain [bɛl ˈkæptən]	服務生領班
suit [sut]	套裝；西裝
press [prɛs]	燙（衣服）

旅遊錦囊

　　在美國住旅館，給服務生小費，一般的情形是每一件行李給二塊美元，如果服務生另外做了其他的服務，如代叫計程車或是送飯菜到房間，還要另外給小費。

心情筆記

Food and Drink

飲食

外國人的飲食與我們完全不同，
所以在外國要吃一頓舒適的飯，
除了要知道正確的英語句型外，
還要知道某些食物的名稱才行。

At Breakfast
早餐

◆ 對話一：準備點菜

朋友一道用餐

旅　客	Do you want tea, or would you rather have coffee? 你要喝茶，還是咖啡？
朋　友	I always have coffee in the morning. 在早上我總是喝咖啡。
旅　客	What are you going to eat? 你打算吃什麼？
朋　友	I'm going to order scrambled eggs and toast. What about you? 我想要點炒蛋和土司。你呢？
旅　客	I'd like bacon and pancakes. 我要培根和薄餅。

◆ 對話二：點飲料

服務員	Would you like anything to drink? 你要喝什麼嗎？
客　人	Coffee, please. 咖啡。
服務員	Sugar and Cream? 要加糖和奶精嗎？
客　人	No, "black" is fine. 不用，純咖啡就行了。

◆ 對話三：點菜

服務員	Ready to order? 要點菜了嗎？
客　人	Yeah. I want the bacon and eggs breakfast. 是，我要培根和煎蛋。
服務員	How do you want your eggs? 你的蛋要幾分熟？
客　人	Over easy. 翻面三分熟。
服務員	What kind of bread? 要那種麵包。

| 客　人 | English muffin, please.
給我英國式鬆餅。 |

◆ 對話四：要煎蛋

客　人	I'll have fried eggs. 我要煎蛋。
服務生	Over or up? 要荷包蛋，還是煎單面？
客　人	Up, please. 煎單面就好。
服務生	How do you want your eggs? 要幾分熟？
客　人	Well-done, please. 全熟。

◆ 對話五：蛋煎得好嗎？

| 服務生 | How do you find your eggs?
你的蛋煎如何？ |
| 客　人 | It's pretty good. Thank you.
很好，謝謝你。 |

→ 問別人要喝什麼飲料，說Would you like anything to drink?或是簡單地問Anything to drink?就行。

→ 煎蛋英文是fried egg，它有兩種煎法，一種是荷包蛋，就是說over，另一種是蛋黃在中間，只煎一面的是sunny-side-up.你點早餐，若點fried egg，服務生會問你，Up or over?就是問你要荷包蛋(over)，或是不要把蛋白翻過去，只煎一面的sunny-side-up。

→ 白煮蛋英文是boiled egg.炒蛋是scrambled egg。

→ 你若點蛋時，服務生還會問你要多熟的？How do you want your eggs?你若要三分熟，是over easy，六、七分熟是medium，十分熟是well done.

要什麼飲料？

❖ Anything to drink?

要喝什麼？

❖ Do you want tea or coffee?

你要茶或咖啡？

❖ What do you want to drink?

你要喝什麼？

❖ You're going to have coffee, aren't you?

你要喝咖啡，是嗎？

❖ You're having coffee, aren't you?

你要喝咖啡，是嗎？

❖ Would you like a cup of coffee?

你要一杯咖啡嗎？

再來一杯

❖ Would you like another cup of coffee?

你還要再來一杯咖啡嗎？

❖ Would you like more tea?

你還要茶嗎？

❖ I want to re-fill my coffee.

我要咖啡續杯。

要吃什麼？

❖ What are you going to eat?

你要什麼？

❖ What do you want?

你要什麼？

❖ Do you want cold cereal or hot cereal?

你要吃冷麥片還是熱麥片？

❖ Do you want toast or would you rather have a roll?

你要土司，還是要小麵包？

❖ I'd like fried eggs.

我要煎蛋。

你要～嗎？

❖ Would you like a cup of coffee?

你要一杯咖啡嗎？

❖ Would you like another cup of coffee?

你要再來一杯咖啡嗎？

❖ Would you like some cream?

你要奶精嗎？

要飲料

❖ I think I'll have a cup of coffee.

我想我要一杯咖啡。

Orange juice, please.

請給我柳橙汁。

點早餐

❖ I'll have scrambled eggs and toast, please.

我要炒蛋和土司。

❖ I'd like an English muffin, please.

我要一份英國式鬆餅。

❖ I think I'll try pancakes and bacon.

我想我要試試薄餅和培根。

❖ I'll have fried eggs.

我要煎蛋。

❖ Give me scrambled eggs, please.

請給我炒蛋。

❖ I'd like fried eggs. sunny-side-up, please.

我要煎蛋，只煎一面的。

❖ I'd like fried eggs. Over, please.

我要煎荷包蛋。

❖ Boiled eggs, please.

請給我白煮蛋。

蛋如何？

❖ How do you want your eggs?

你的蛋要幾分熟？

❖ How do you find your eggs?

蛋做的還可以嗎？

再要東西

❖ May I have some more cream, please?

請再給我一些奶精。

❖ Please bring more butter to me.

請再給我一些奶油。

 重要單字

toast [tost]	土司
French toast	法國土司
roll [rol]	小麵包
muffin [ˈmʌfɪn]	英國鬆餅
donut [ˈdonət]	甜甜圈
pancake [ˈpænkek]	薄餅
waffle [ˈwɑfl]	鬆餅
cereal [ˈsɪrɪəl]	麥片粥
fried egg [fraɪd]	煎蛋
sunny-side up [ˈsʌnɪ saɪd ʌp]	只煎一面的煎蛋
scrambled egg [ˌskræmbl̩d ˈɛg]	炒蛋
boiled egg [bɔɪld ˈɛg]	白煮蛋
over-easy [ˈovɚ ˈizɪ]	蛋煎三分熟
medium [ˈmidɪəm]	蛋煎五分熟
over medium	蛋煎八分熟
well-done	蛋煎全熟
bacon [ˈbekən]	培根
ham	火腿
sausage [ˈsɔsɪdʒ]	香腸

Chapter 5

Unit 2

At Lunch
午餐

◆ 對話一：吃午餐

朋　友	Do you want another hamburger or more French fries? 你要再來一客漢堡或是一些薯條嗎？
旅　客	Thank you, but I really can't eat any more. 謝謝你，但我實在是吃不下了。

◆ 對話二：飯後甜點

朋　友	Would you like some more soup? 你還要一些湯嗎？。
旅　客	No, thanks. I'm supposed to be on a diet. 不，謝謝，我正在節食。
朋　友	Why don't we have something for dessert? 我們何不吃一些甜點？
旅　客	I really shouldn't, but I'll have a small piece of pie. 我實在不該吃，但我還是要一小片派好了。

◆ 對話三：吃飽了

朋　友	Do you want any dessert? 你要甜點嗎？
旅　客	No, thank you. I'm really full. 不，謝謝，我很飽了。

 句型分析

→ 用餐時，問Would you like some more～?表示對方已經吃過某樣東西，你問他還要不要再來一些？但若是還沒吃過，你問對方要不要來一些，就不要more，只要問Would you like some ～?就可以。

→ 回答說，不想再吃了，可用以下幾種說法：No, thanks. I'm full.就是I just can't eat any more。就是I've had enough.

 句型練習

吃甜點

❖ Why don't we have something for dessert?
我們何不吃一點甜點？

❖ Would you like some dessert?
你要一些甜點嗎？。

❖ Aren't you going to have dessert?

你不要甜點嗎？。

❖ How about a piece of apple pie for dessert?

要不要一片蘋果派當甜點？

吃不下了

❖ It's very delicious, but I really shouldn't have any more.

很好吃，但我實在不該再吃了。

❖ No, thanks. I'm supposed to be on a diet.

不，謝謝，我正在節食。

❖ No, thanks. I've had enough.

不，謝謝，我吃得很飽了。

❖ No, thanks. I've had too much.

不，謝謝，我吃得太多了。

❖ No, thanks. I'm full.

不，謝謝，我已飽了。

sandwich	三明治
soup [sup]	湯
ice cream	冰淇淋
delicious [dɪˈlɪʃəs]	好吃
yummy [ˈjʌmɪ]	好吃（小孩式說法）
on a diet	節食
dessert [dɪˈzɝt]	甜點
apple pie	蘋果派

旅遊錦囊

　　美國人吃早餐，麵包類有roll, toast, French toast, muffin, waffle, pancake和biscuit等，看中文翻譯，還是不知道那是什麼，最好是有機會實際品嚐一番。

　　美國人飯後有吃甜點的習慣，所以在飯後問美國朋友要不要再吃一點甜點，是很受用的，常見的甜點包括各種水果派，蛋糕和冰淇淋。

　　美國人吃飯，通常都會有一杯飲料在旁，你若不喜歡任何飲料，儘管叫冰水就行，記住冰水是iced water.不是ice water.因為加了冰，所以ice是當動詞，再改成iced，文法上叫做「過去分詞當形容詞用，表示被動」。

Unit 3

At Dinner
晚餐

◆ 對話一：剛入座

服務生	Can I get you anything to drink? 你要喝什麼嗎？
旅　客	Yes, please. I think I'll have orange juice. 好的，我想我要柳橙汁。
服務生	Are you ready to order? 你可以點菜了嗎？
旅　客	No, not yet. We need a little more time. 不，還沒，我們需要一點時間。
服務生	O.K. I'll come back in a few minutes. 好的，我一會兒再來。

◆ 對話二：點菜

服務生	May I take your order now? 你們可以點菜了。

旅　客	Yes, I'd like steak dinner, and I'd like mashed potato instead of French fries. 好，我要牛排餐，還有，我要馬鈴薯泥，不要薯條。
服務生	How do you want your steak? 你的牛排要幾分熟的。
旅　客	Medium, please. 六、七分熟。
服務生	Would you like salad or soup with that? 你要沙拉或是湯？。
旅　客	Salad with French dressing. 沙拉，要法國沙拉醬。
服務生	Roll or garlic bread? 小麵包還是大蒜麵包？
旅　客	Roll. 小麵包。

（服務生對朋友……）

服務生	All right. And you, miss? 好的，妳呢？小姐？
朋　友	I'll have a roast beef sandwich. 我要烤牛肉三明治。
服務生	O.K. 好。

Chapter 5

◆ 對話三：服務生上菜

服務生 You had the roast beef sandwich, right?
你點了牛肉三明治，是嗎？

朋　友 Yes, it's mine.
是的，那是我的。

（服務生對旅客……）

服務生 And here you are. Enjoy your meal.
這是你的，好好享受你們的晚餐。

旅　客 Thank you.　By the way, do you have any Tabasco sauce?
謝謝你，還有，你們有辣椒醬嗎？

服務生 Yes, we do. I'll bring some right away.
有，我們有，我馬上拿給你。

◆ 對話四：服務生的服務

服務生 Is everything O.K.?
一切都好嗎？

旅　客 Yes, everything's fine.
是的，都很好。

服務生 Can I get you anything else?
你還要其他東西嗎？

旅　客	Well, could you bring us a few napkins? 嗯，你可以拿幾張紙巾來嗎？
服務生	Sure. 好的。
旅　客	And could we have the check, please? 還有，請拿帳單給我們。
服務生	Yes, of course. 好的。

句型分析

→ 在美國除了速食餐廳外，一般餐廳在剛進門處都會有個牌子寫 "Please wait to be seated." seat 當名詞指座位，在這兒當動詞用，加be在前面，be seated表被動式，就是說你要等著被帶入座。

→ 服務生帶你入座後，通常會先問你要什麼飲料，你可以簡單的說你要的飲料，例如：Orange juice, iced water。當然你也可以用本課的句型，I think I'll have orange juice.

→ 服務生來問你要點菜沒？你若還沒決定點什麼，就告訴服務生We need a little more time.

服務生接受點菜

❖ Are you ready to order?

你要點菜了嗎？

❖ May I take your order now?

你們要點菜了嗎？

❖ Would you like to order now?

你們現在要點菜了嗎？

❖ Have you decided what you'd like?

你們決定點什麼了嗎？

點菜

❖ I'd like to see the menu again.

我要再看一次菜單。

❖ I'll have a steak, medium rare.

我要牛排，五分熟。

❖ I think I'll try the turkey.

我想我要試試火雞。

❖ I'd like soup instead of salad.

我要湯，不要沙拉。

向服務生要東西

❖ Do you have any ketchup?

你們有蕃茄醬嗎？

❖ Would you bring us a few napkins, please?

請拿一些紙巾給我們，好嗎？

結帳

❖ Would I have the check, please?

請給我帳單，好嗎？

❖ I'd like to have the check, please.

我要帳單。

❖ Waiter, give me the check, please.

服務生，請給我帳單。

 重要單字

drink	喝（飲料）
iced water [aɪst ˈwɑtɚ]	冰水
restaurant [ˈrɛstərənt]	餐廳
today's special [təˈdez ˈspɛʃəl]	今日特餐
menu [ˈmɛnjʊ]	菜單
order	點菜
napkin [ˈnæpkɪn]	紙巾

check	帳單
rare [rɛr]	牛排三分熟
medium	牛排五分熟
over medium	牛排七分熟
well done	牛排全熟
salad dressing [ˌsæləd ˈdrɛsɪŋ]	沙拉醬
steak sauce [ˈstek sɔs]	牛排醬
ketchup [ˈkɛtʃəp]	蕃茄醬
hot sauce	辣椒醬
spicy [ˈspaɪsɪ]	辣的
Tabasco sauce [təˈbæsko]	辣椒醬
appetizer [ˈæpətaɪzɚ]	小菜
steak dinner [stek ˈdɪnɚ]	牛排餐
roast chicken [rost ˈtʃɪkən]	烤雞
fried shrimp [fraɪd ʃrɪmp]	炸蝦
baked potato [bekt pəˈteto]	烤馬鈴薯
garlic bread [ˌgɑrlɪk ˈbrɛd]	蒜味麵包
roast beef sandwich	烤牛肉三明治

Unit 4

At Fast-food Restaurant
在速食餐廳

◆ 對話一:點菜

服務生	May I help you? 你需要什麼嗎?
旅 客	I'd like Bacon cheeseburger and large fries. 我要培根乳酪漢堡和大包的薯條。
服務生	Anything to drink? 要喝什麼嗎?
旅 客	A large Coke. 一杯大杯的可樂。
服務生	Is that all? 就這些嗎?
旅 客	Yes. 是的。
服務生	For here or to go. 在這兒吃還是帶走。

旅　客	For here. 在這兒吃。

→ 到速食廳，很多人是買了就走，所以，服務生通常會問你一句，For here or to go.也就是說你要在這裡吃，還是要帶走。

→ 在美國的速食餐廳點可樂，就得直接講要large, medium或small的coke就行。千萬別說你要a cup of coke,因為美國人不這樣說，美國人都說，要a large coke或a medium coke,你若說a cup of coke,服務生的腦筋一下子會轉不過來。

點飲料

❖ Can I get you anything to drink?

你喝什麼？

❖ I'd like a medium Coke.

我要中杯的可樂。

點薯條

❖ Large fries to go, please.

大包的薯條，帶走的。

❖ I'd like a small fries.

我要小包的薯條。

 重要單字

French fries [frɛntʃ ˈfraɪz]	薯條
fried chicken [fraɪd ˈtʃɪkən]	炸雞
pizza [ˈpɪzɑ]	比薩餅
hot dog	熱狗
sandwich	三明治
soft drink	冷飲
hamburger [ˈhæmbɚgɚ]	漢堡
bacon cheeseburger [ˈbekən ˈtʃizbɚgɚ]	培根乳酪漢堡

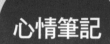

心情筆記

In the Department Store

在百貨公司

到美國，在百貨公司購物是觀光必需的一環，
如何與店員溝通，
如何退換物品，
請注意以下的句型。

Unit 1

May I help you?
你需要什麼嗎？

◆ 對話一：店員提供服務

店　員	May I help you? 你需要什麼嗎？
顧　客	No, I'm just looking. 不，我只是到處看看。
店　員	If you find anything you like, just let me know. 如果你找到你喜歡的，只需告訴我一聲。

◆ 對話二：詢問尺寸

店　員	Are you being helped? 有人在為你服務嗎？
顧　客	No. I'm looking for blue suits. 沒有，我在找藍色的套裝。
店　員	What size do you wear? 你穿幾號的？

顧　客	A six. 六號。
店　員	The closest I have is an 8. 我現在有的最接近的是八號。
顧　客	Do you think you'll be getting any more in? 你想你們會很快再進貨嗎？
店　員	No, but they might have them at our other stores. 不會，但你可以到我們其他的分店去找找看。

◆ 對話三：買泳衣

店　員	May I help you? 你需要什麼嗎？
顧　客	I'd like to see some bathing suits, please. 我想看泳衣。
店　員	Well, we have some beautiful ones. 嗯，我們有一些漂亮的泳衣。
	I'm sure we have one just for you. 我確定我們一定有你要的。
	What size do you wear? 你穿幾號？

句型分析

→ 在百貨公司，店員問你需要什麼時，通常都是問May I help you?但店員若不確定是否已有別的店員在為你服務時，則會用Are you being helped?這裡的be helped用被動式，問你有沒有被服務，再改成現在進行式，Are you being helped?

→ 當你要的東西該店正好沒貨時，你就會問他們，是否很快會進貨，記住這個句子，Will you be getting any more in?

→ close這個字，在本課指尺寸的接近。the closest I have 意思是「我有的最接近的尺寸」，I have是形容詞子句，在說明the closest，完整的句型是the closest that I have is 8，在口語中that通常省略。

句型練習

提供服務

❖ May I help you?

你需要什麼嗎？

❖ May I help you find anything?

你需要我幫你的忙嗎？

❖ Are you being helped?

有人為你服務嗎？

❖ Is anyone waiting on you?

有人在為你服務嗎？

❖ Are you looking for anything particular to buy?

你要找什麼特別的東西嗎？

回答店員的提議

❖ I'm just looking.

我只是看看。

❖ I'm just looking around.

我只是到處看看。

❖ Yes, I'm being waited on, thank you.

是的，有人在為我服務了，謝謝。

❖ Yes, someone is helping me, thank you.

是的，已有人在幫我的忙，謝謝。

告訴店員欲購的項目

❖ I'm looking for blue skirts.

我在找藍色的裙子。

❖ I'm trying to find suits in size 8.

我在找八號的套裝。

❖ I'd like a long-sleeved shirt to match the suits.

我要一件長袖襯衫配這件套裝。

❖ I'd like to see some bathing suits, please.

我要看看泳衣。

❖ Do you have something like this one, in size 10?

像這件的，你們有沒有十號的。

沒有合適的尺寸

❖ The closest I have is a 12.

我現有的最接近的尺寸是12號。

❖ We have your size, but not in that color.

我們有你要的尺寸，但沒有那個顏色。

❖ I'm afraid we're out of your size.

你要的尺寸，我們已沒貨了。

❖ I think we don't have any left.

我想都賣光了。

❖ I'm sorry, but size 8 is the smallest I have in stock.

對不起，但是8號是我現有最小的尺寸。

❖ The smallest I have is this one.

我有的最小的是這件。

穿幾號？

❖ What size do you wear?

你穿幾號的？

會再進貨嗎？

❖ Will you be getting any more in?

你還會再多進一些嗎？

 重要單字

mall [mɔl]	大型購物中心
department store [dɪˈpɑrtmənt stor]	百貨公司
suit [sut]	套裝
size	尺寸；大小
wear	穿；戴

Unit 2

Trying on
試穿

◆ 對話一：要試穿衣服

顧　客	Ma'am? ... I'd like to try on the sweaters. 這位女士？……我想試穿這些毛衣。
	Where are the fitting rooms? 請問試衣室在那裏？
店　員	They are over there. 在那邊。
顧　客	Thank you. 謝謝你。

◆ 對話二：試穿後

店　員	How was the suit? 這件套裝如何？
顧　客	Well, the waist of the skirt was a little tight. 嗯，裙子的腰圍有點太緊。
	Could I try a larger size? 我可以試大一號的。

| 店　員 | Certainly.
當然可以。 |

◆ 對話三：試穿另一件之後

店　員	What do you think of that one? 那一件你認為怎麼樣？
顧　客	It seems a little big. 好像有點太大。
店　員	Are you sure?　It looks good on you. 會嗎？你穿起來很好看。
	Here, this blouse goes with it. 拿去，這件上衣配那件套裝。
	Try it on. 試穿一下。

◆ 對話四：試穿後

店　員	How was the jacket? 這件夾克如何？
顧　客	Well, it's too small. 嗯，太小了。
店　員	Would you like to try a larger size? 你要不要試穿大一號的？

Chapter 6

顧 客	No, it's not the right style. 不用了，款式也不對。
	It seems a little old-fashioned. 看起來太老式了。
店 員	Well, what about the pants....? 那，褲子如何呢？

◆ 對話五：花色不喜歡

店 員	How do you like it? 你喜不喜歡？
顧 客	I don't like all those flowers. 我不喜歡那麼多花。
	They are too loud. 太雜了。
店 員	But that's the style this year. 但那是今年流行的款式。

◆ 對話六：再試其他衣服

店 員	How about those over there? 那邊那幾件怎麼樣？
顧 客	They look old-fashioned. 看起來太老式了。

店 員	Well, do you like this one?
	那，你喜歡這件嗎？

顧 客	Hmm... that one is not bad.
	那件還好。

	What do you think?
	你認為如何？

店 員	It's very nice. You should like it.
	那件很好，你會喜歡它。

顧 客	How much is it?
	多少錢？

店 員	$8,000.00
	八千塊。

顧 客	Oh, no, that's too expensive.
	哦，不，太貴了。

◆ 對話七：找到喜歡的衣服

店 員	What do you think?
	你認為如何？

店 員	The style is very flattering on you.
	這個款式你穿起來很好看。

店 員	You really like it?
	你真的喜歡嗎？

顧 客	Sure. 當然。

顧 客	O.K. I'll take it. 好吧，那我就買了。

句型分析

→ 問人家的意見，問她覺得某件東西如何？有兩種問法，
How is～?或What do you think of～?

→ 說一件東西「好像～」，英文句型是It seems後面加形
容詞，如 too big , too tight , too small 等等。

→ 說一件衣服穿在某人身上很好看，用flattering這個形容
詞，例如：The dress is flattering on you.

→ 說某件東西的價錢真的很便宜，不要用cheap這個字。
cheap含有東西不值錢的意思。用It's a good buy.或
It's a bargain.表示以那樣的價錢，買到這件東西真是便
宜。

→ You really like it?（你真的喜歡嗎？）是一句口語上用
的疑問句，在句尾把語調提高。它跟Do you like it?（你
喜不喜歡？）意思不一樣。

問意見時

❖ How was the suit?

那件套裝如何？

❖ How were the suits?

那幾件套裝如何？

❖ What do you think of the suit?

你認為這件套裝如何？

❖ How do you like it?

你喜歡嗎？

❖ Does the sweater fit?

毛衣合身嗎？

表示意見

❖ It's not very comfortable.

它不太舒服。

❖ It's just right.

它恰好合適。

❖ It's too tight.

它太緊了。

❖ It feels loose.

它太鬆了。

❖ It seems a little old-fashioned.

它太老式了。

❖ It seems too big.

似乎太大了。

價錢合理否？

❖ It's a very good buy.

這個價錢很好。

❖ It's too expensive.

它太貴了。

❖ It's a bargain.

這個很便宜。

形式合適嗎？

❖ It looks good on you.

你穿起來很好看。

❖ The style is very flattering on you.

這個形式你穿起來很好看。

❖ That's the style this year.

那是今年流行的形式。

❖ The style is in fashion.

那個形式是流行的形式。

重要單字

skirt [skɝt]	裙子
sweater [ˈswɛtɚ]	毛衣
slacks [slæks]	西褲
pants [pænts]	長褲
shirt [ʃɝt]	襯衫
blouse [blaʊs]	女上衣
T-shirt	T恤
waist [west]	腰圍
style [staɪl]	形式
in fashion [ɪn ˈfæʃən]	流行的
in style	流行的
old-fashioned [old ˈfæʃənd]	老式的
flatter [ˈflætɚ]	奉承
fit [fɪt]	合身
loose [lus]	鬆的
tight [taɪt]	緊的
loud [laʊd]	太鮮豔
comfortable [ˈkʌmfɚtəbl]	舒服
bargain [ˈbɑrgən]	好價錢
expensive [ɪksˈpɛnsɪv]	貴的

Unit 3

Paying and Refunding
付款和退換

◆ 對話一：走近收銀處

| 店 員 | Hi, do you find everything O.K.?
嗨，一切都好嗎？ |
| 顧 客 | Yes, thank you.
是的，謝謝你。 |

◆ 對話二：付款方式

店 員	Will that be cash or charge? 要用現金還是刷卡？
顧 客	Cash. Do you take an out-of-state check? 現金，你們收外州支票嗎？
店 員	No, I'm sorry. 不收，對不起。
顧 客	That's fine. I'll get some cash from the ATM around the corner. 沒關係，我到轉角處的提款機去領現款。

	Would you hold this suit for me? 可否幫我把這件套裝留著？
	I'll be back soon. 我一會兒就回來。
店　員	Sure. I'll hold it for you. 好的，我會幫你留著。

◆ 對話三：包裝禮物

顧　客	This is a wedding gift for a friend. 這是給朋友的結婚禮物。
	Do you have a service counter to wrap it up for me? 你們店裏有服務處可以幫我把它包裝起來嗎？
店　員	Yes. Go down the aisle. You'll see the service counter on the right. 有的，從這條走道走下去，在你的右邊你會看到服務處。

◆ 對話四：退換

顧客	I want to return the suit. 我要退還這件套裝。
店　員	Do you have the receipt? 你有收據嗎？

顧　客	Yes, I bought it here yesterday, but it was too small. 有的，我昨天在這裡買的，但是太小了。
店　員	Do you want an exchange? 你要換一件嗎？
顧　客	No, I need a refund. 不要，我要退錢。

◆ 對話五：找不到欲購物品

店　員	How can I help you? 有什麼事嗎？
顧　客	I saw it on today's paper that Sony stereos are on sale. 我看到今天報紙廣告說新力牌音響在打折。
店　員	Yes, that's right. 是的，沒錯。
顧　客	But I can't find any on the shelf. 但是我在架子上找不到。
店　員	If there aren't any on the shelf, they are out of stock. 如果架子上沒有，那就是賣完了。
顧　客	May I have the rain check then? 那我可不可以要一張「預約單」。

句型分析

→ 購物時，若你看中某樣物品，但身上正好錢不夠，你想請店員幫你留著，別讓別人買去了，可以説Would you hold it for me?在這兒hold不是拿著的意思，而是放在一旁，留著的意思。

→ 如果打折的物品賣完了，你可以向店裏要一張rain check，等有貨時，可以用打折的價錢買到該物品。

句型練習

結帳

❖ Will that be cash or charge?

要用現金還是刷卡。

❖ Will that be Sear's charge card?

要用席爾斯的簽帳卡付嗎？

❖ Cash or charge?

要用現金還是刷卡？

❖ Do you take an out-of-state check?

你們收外州支票嗎？

❖ Do you take travelers checks?

你們收旅行支票嗎？

❖ Do you take personal checks?

你們收私人支票嗎？

退換

❖ Do you have a receipt?

你有收據嗎？

❖ Do you need a refund?

你要退錢嗎？

❖ Do you want an exchange?

你要換一件嗎？

❖ I want to return the sweater.

我要退這件毛衣。

❖ I want to exchange the pants for a larger size.

我要換一件大一號的長褲。

重要單字

gift	禮物
wedding gift	結婚禮物
wrap [ræp]	包裝
service counter [ˌsɝvɪs ˈkaʊntɚ]	服務台
aisle [aɪl]	走道
shelf [ʃɛlf]	架子

pay	付款
receipt [rɪˈsit]	收據
refund [rɪˈfʌnd]	退款
exchange [ɪksˈtʃendʒ]	交換
return	退還
cash [kæʃ]	現金
charge [tʃɑrdʒ]	收費
charge card	簽帳卡
personal check	私人支票
out-of-state check	外州支票
on sale	打折
out of stock [ˈaut əv stɑk]	沒存貨
rain check [ˈren tʃɛk]	預約單

旅遊錦囊

　　在美國租車，如果沒有信用卡的話，租車行通常會要你付一筆押金，才肯把車租給你。說到信用卡，你會聽到對方問你有沒有major credit cards，為何信用卡還要加個major呢？對方的意思是問你有沒有Master，Visa或American Express，這三種是美國最大的信用卡。其他的信用卡，如Discover他們有的不收。

At a Shoe Store
在鞋店

◆ 對話一：計畫去買鞋

旅　　客	I need to go get a new pair of shoes today. 我今天要去買雙新鞋子。
外國人	Oh, really? 噢,真的嗎?
	What are you looking for? 你要買什麼鞋子?
旅　　客	I need a pair of jogging shoes. Mine are worn out. 我需要一雙慢跑鞋。我那一雙已破了。
外國人	I need a new pair of athletic shoes, too. 我也需要一雙運動鞋。
	Can I go with you? 我可以跟你一起去嗎?

店　員	May I help you? 有什麼事嗎？
顧　客	I'd like to see those shoes. 我要看看那些鞋子。
店　員	These? 這些嗎？
顧　客	No, the ones next to the black heels. 不是，是在黑色高跟鞋旁邊那些。
店　員	Oh, those. 噢，是那些。

句型分析

→　sale可以是拍賣，也可以是銷售。如何分辨，請看下面例句：

① John made ten dollars on the sale of his bicycle.（銷售）約翰賣他的腳踏車賺了十元。

② The store is having a sale on clothing.（拍賣）那家店在打折拍賣衣服。

③ for sale（銷售）How long has the car been for sale?這部車子賣多久了？

④ on sale（打折拍賣）Are the coats on sale?這些大衣在打折拍賣嗎？

句型練習

鞋子的尺寸

❖ What size shoes do you wear?

你穿幾號的鞋子。

❖ I wear a size 8.

我穿八號的。

打折中

❖ The tennis shoes are on sale. They're 20% off.

運動鞋在打折,是八折優待。

❖ When does the sale begin?

打折從什麼時候開始?

❖ When does the sale end?

打折什麼時候結束?

❖ Are the sneakers on sale?

布鞋在打折嗎?。

casual shoes [ˈkæʒjʊəl]	便鞋
sneakers [ˈsnikɚz]	布鞋
athletic shoes [æθˈlɛtɪk]	運鞋
jogging shoes [ˈdʒɑgɪn]	慢跑鞋
jelly shoes [ˈdʒɛlɪ]	塑膠鞋
boots	馬靴
heels [hilz]	鞋跟
chunky heels [ˈtʃʌŋkɪ]	大後跟的鞋子
high heels	高跟鞋
low heels	低跟鞋

旅遊錦囊

　　當你買完東西，在結帳時，店員會問你，"paper or plastic"，有時你會一時摸不著頭緒。原來，店員是要幫你把東西用袋子裝起來，他問你要用紙袋子還是塑膠袋子。

　　aisle這個字，在觀光英語裏常見到，它用在兩種情形，一是坐飛機時，指靠走道的座位，説aisle seat。另一是在超級市場內，貨架東西是一排排放，所以每兩排貨架中間的走道也叫aisle，第一排走道叫aisle one，第二排叫aisle two，以此類推。在百貨公司內也有aisle，讓你沿著它走。

For Cosmetics

採購化粧品

◆ 對話一：買唇膏、粉底

店　員	How can I help you today? 你今天要買什麼嗎？
顧　客	I want to buy the foundation and the lipstick. 我要買粉底和唇膏。
店　員	What color do you have in mind for them? 你知道你要買什麼色澤嗎？
顧　客	I'd like natural beige for the foundation. 粉底我要自然膚色。
	But, the lipstick... I'm not sure what color I'd buy. 但是，唇膏嗎……我還沒確定要買什麼顏色。
	Could you show me some with brighter color? 你可以給我看一些比較亮麗的顏色嗎？
店　員	How about this? It's "Firecracker". 這個如何？是火焰色。

| 顧　客 | Well, I think a shade darker may be better.
嗯，我想再暗一點的色澤可能會較好。 |

◆ 對話二：買化粧水

顧　客	Hi, I want to buy toner. 嗨，我要買化粧水。
店　員	We have two kinds. 我有兩種。
	The one with light purple bottle is for normal to dry skin. 紫色瓶子是給中性偏乾性的皮膚。
	And the one with light blue bottle is for normal to oily skin. 淡藍色瓶子是給中性偏油性的皮膚。
	Which one do you want? 你要那一種？

◆ 對話3三：買粉

| 店　員 | May I help you?
有什麼事嗎？ |
| 顧　客 | Yes, what shade of powder should I use for my skin tone?
是的，依我的膚色，應該買那種色澤的粉？ |

店 員	Let's see... Your skin complexion is a little darker. 讓我看看……你的膚色稍黑。
	The shade of "medium" would be the best. 中色系列能最好。

◆ 對話四：專櫃化粧品

店 員	May I help you? 有什麼事嗎？
顧 客	Yes, I'm looking for cosmetics of Estee Lauder. 是的，我在找雅詩蘭黛的化粧品。
店 員	We don't carry the products of Estee Lauder. 我們不賣雅詩蘭黛的產品。
顧 客	Do you know which department store in the mall carries them? 你知道那家百貨公司賣嗎？
店 員	You may try Macy's. 你可以試試梅西百貨公司。
	I think they have counters for Estee Lauder. 我想他們有雅詩蘭黛的專櫃。

店　員	My wife wanted me to buy some cosmetics for her. 我太太要我買一些化粧品給她。
顧　客	What brand does she prefer? 她要什麼品牌的？
店　員	What do you suggest? 你有什麼建議？
顧　客	You may try Elizabeth Arden. Arden has great products. 你可以買伊莉莎白雅頓的，雅頓的產品很好。
店　員	I remember that my wife mentioned the brand "Mary Kay". 我記得我太太提過玫琳凱這個品牌。
顧　客	The products of "Mary Kay" are by direct sale. 玫琳凱的產品是直銷的。
店　員	Well, then. I'll buy some from Elizabeth Arden. 那，我買伊莉沙白雅頓的。

Chapter 6

- ✈ 表示較喜歡，用prefer，例如：I prefer to study in the library.（我較喜歡在圖書館讀書。）Which one do you prefer?（你較喜歡那一樣？）

- ✈ 如果有兩樣東西，較喜歡其中一樣時，說prefer～to～。John prefers football to baseball.（約翰較喜歡足球，不喜歡棒球），接在prefer之後的東西，即是較喜歡的那個。

句型練習

化粧品的色澤

❖ What shade of foundation should I use for my skin tone?

依我的膚色，我該買那種色澤的粉底？

❖ You have a very light complexion.

你的膚色很白。

❖ You have a very dark complexion.

你的膚色很黑。

❖ Do you have lipsticks a shade lighter?

你有沒有色澤淡一點的唇膏。

❖ I like the color of your lipstick.

我喜歡你唇膏的顏色。

化粧品的品牌

❖ What brand do you prefer?

你較喜歡那種品牌？

❖ What's your preference for the brand?

你較喜歡那種品牌？

❖ What's your preference for the shade of the lipsticks?

你較喜歡那種唇膏的色澤？

❖ What do you suggest?

你有什麼建議？

 重要單字

toner [ˈtonɚ]	化粧水
lotion [ˈloʃən]	化粧乳液
cream [krim]	保養乳液
foundation [faʊnˈdeʃən]	粉底
powder [ˈpaʊdɚ]	粉
eye shadow [ˌaɪˈʃedo]	眼影
blush [blʌʃ]	腮紅
lipstick [ˈlɪpstɪk]	唇膏
shade [ʃed]	色澤
skin tone [skɪn ton]	膚色
skin complexion [skɪn kəmˈplɛkʃən]	膚色
cosmetics [kɑzˈmɛtɪks]	化粧品

counter [ˈkaʊntɚ]	專櫃
prefer [prɪˈfɝ]	較喜歡
brand	品牌
product [ˈprɑdʌkt]	產品
direct sale [dəˈrɛkt sel]	直銷

旅遊錦囊

在百貨公司購物，要結帳時，店員會問你
Cash or charge? 她是問你要付現金，還是刷卡。如果
你決定用其中一樣，就直接回答店員。但你若是想用旅
行支票付錢，別慌，只要告訴店員，Travelers check.就行
了。另外，有些百貨公司自己發行簽帳下，為了要大家多使
用它們的卡，店員故意不問你cash or charge，而是問你是不
是要用該百貨公司的卡結帳。你只要說No，就行了。

試穿室叫fitting room，你若想試穿衣服時，可以問店員
Where are the fitting rooms?

在美國購物，大部分的物品，都是可以退換的，但你一
定要把receipt（收據）收好，沒有receipt要退換就難了。

如果某件打折物品賣完了，你可以向店員要rain
check，拿著rain check，改天該物品不打折時，你仍然
可以用打折時的價錢購買，可以省很多錢噢！

In the Supermarket

在超級市場

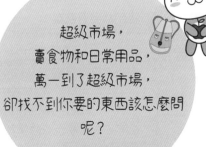

超級市場，
賣食物和日常用品，
萬一到了超級市場，
卻找不到你要的東西該怎麼問
呢？

Unit 1

Shopping List
購物單

◆ 對話一：擬購物單

旅客A	What do we need from the supermarket? 到超級市場要買什麼？
旅客B	We need vegetables. 我們需要買蔬菜。
旅客A	Do we need fruit? 我們需要水果嗎？
旅客B	Yes, I'd like a few apples and pears. 是的，我想要一些蘋果和梨子。
旅客A	Any meat? 要肉嗎？
旅客B	Yes. Three pounds of ground beef and a whole chicken. 要，三磅絞牛肉和一隻雞。
旅客A	Anything else? 還要什麼嗎？

旅客B	Get some donuts from the bakery . 在糕餅部買一些甜甜圈。

◆ 對話二：問東西在那？

顧　客	Excuse me. Where's the milk? 對不起，牛奶放那裏？
店　員	Down at aisle 12 in the dairy section. 從12號走道下去，在乳酪部。
顧　客	Thanks. By the way, where's the fruit? 謝謝，那水果呢？
店　員	In the produce section at the corner of the store. When you're through, the check-out stand is over there. 在店裏的角落處，蔬果部，還有等你買完了，結帳櫃台就在那裏。
顧　客	Thanks a lot. 謝謝。

◆ 對話三：問東西放在那裏？

顧　客	Excuse me. Can you tell me where the cake mixes are? 對不起，你能告訴蛋糕粉放那兒嗎？

| 店　員 | Yes, there're on aisle 7, on the bottom shelf, next to sugar.
可以，就在第七排走道，在最下面的架子，就在糖的旁邊。 |

店　員 Yes, there're on aisle 7, on the bottom shelf, next to sugar.
可以，就在第七排走道，在最下面的架子，就在糖的旁邊。

◆ 對話四：討論品牌

顧　客 We need peanut butter.
我們需要花生醬。

店　員 What brand do you prefer?
你較喜歡什麼牌？

顧　客 Let's buy the store brand. It's cheaper.
我們買店裏自己的品牌，那較便宜。

店　員 But more people buy the "Skippy" brand than the store brand.
但是大部份人買「史基皮」的品牌。

There must be a reason.
應該是有原因的。

顧　客 I don't think there is much difference.
我認為差別不大。

→ 超級市場內，食品分部門擺置，你必須知道各部門的英語怎麼說，萬一要問店員時，才不會有雞同鴨講的情形。肉類(meat section)；乳酪類是(dairy section)；蔬果類是(produce section)；糕餅類是(bakery)。

→ 超級市場內，有一處叫deli，這個字全名是delicatessen，我們叫它熟食部，該處是賣煮好的肉類、沙拉、香腸、燻魚等。

→ Excuse me.和I'm sorry.這兩句話，中文翻譯都是「對不起」或「很抱歉」，實際上，這兩句話有不同的用法。Excuse me.有抱歉、打擾的意思，用在問路或請人家讓路借過時，而I'm sorry.則真正有道歉的意思，你若不小心撞到人時，用I'm sorry.。

句型練習

問東西放那裏？

❖ Excuse me. Where's the produce section?

對不起，請問蔬果類在那裏？

❖ Excuse me. Can you tell me where the butter is?

對不起，請問奶油放在那裏？

❖ When you're through, let me know.

等你買完了，告訴我一聲。

supermarket [ˌsjupɚˈmɑrkɪt]	超級市場
pear [pɛr]	梨子
pound	磅
ground beef [ˈɡraʊnd bif]	絞牛肉
ground pork	絞豬肉
whole [hol]	整個角落
corner [ˈkɔrnɚ]	角落
cake mix	蛋糕粉
bottom [ˈbɑtəm]	底下
shelf	架子
peanut butter	花生醬
brand [brænd]	品牌
butter	奶油
vegetable [ˈvɛdʒɪtəbl̩]	蔬菜
bakery [ˈbekərɪ]	糕餅部
aisle [aɪl]	走道
check-out stand	結帳櫃台
dairy section [ˌdɛrɪ ˈsɛkʃən]	乳酪部
produce section [prəˈdjus]	蔬果部

Unit 2

Buying Fruit
買水果

◆ 對話一：買太多水果

旅客A	Look at all these tomatoes. 看看這些蕃茄。
	How many pounds did you buy? 你買了幾磅？
旅客B	Six. 六磅。
旅客A	Six pounds! You know I don't like tomatoes. 六磅！你明知道我不喜歡蕃茄的。
	I never eat them. 我從不吃蕃茄。
	Why did you buy so many? 你為何買那麼多？
旅客B	Because they were on sale, three pounds for a dollar. 因為蕃茄在打折，三磅才美金一塊錢。

◆ 對話二：罐頭水果

旅客A	Don't buy canned peaches. 不要買罐頭桃子。
	I always eat fresh fruit. 我總是吃新鮮水果。
旅客B	But canned peaches taste better. 但是罐頭桃子較好吃。
	And they are cheaper, too. 而且也較便宜。
旅客A	When it's in season, fresh produce is cheaper. 如果是應時的話，鮮果較便宜。

◆ 對話三：挑選水果

旅客A	I want to buy a watermelon. 我要買一個西瓜。
旅客B	Be careful. Don't buy a damaged one. 小心點，別買碰壞的。
旅客A	Hey, the plums look delicious. 嗨，李子看起來很好吃。
	Let's pick some. 我們去挑一些。
旅客B	Don't pick pieces that are too ripe, or not ripe enough. 別挑太熟的，或不夠熟的。

→ check out（結算），用在付款或登記以便離開，如在超級市場結帳，在旅館結算房錢，或是在圖書館向館員登記借書時，都是check out。

→ check in有報到、登記註冊的意思。如坐飛機，要到機場向航空公司櫃台check in，或是要住旅館，要在櫃台check in。

句型練習

買水果

❖ Buy fruit that is in season.

要買應時的水果。

❖ If you buy fruit that is in season, it will be cheaper.

如果你買應時的水果，會便宜些。

❖ Keep fresh fruit in the vegetable bin in the refrigerator.

把鮮果放在冰箱的蔬菜箱內。

❖ Fresh fruit spoils quickly. Don't buy more than we need.

鮮果壞的快，別買多於我們吃得下的。

❖ When you pick fruits, don't squeeze.

挑水果時，別用力擠。

carrot ['kærət]	紅蘿蔔
tomato	蕃茄
onion ['ʌnjən]	洋蔥
celery ['sɛlərɪ]	芹菜
apple	蘋果
pear [pɛr]	梨子
lemon	檸檬
canned fruit [kænd]	罐頭食品
frozen food ['frozən fud]	冰凍食物
fresh [frɛʃ]	新鮮的
taste [test]	嚐起來
in season	應時
damaged ['dæmɪdʒɪd]	碰壞的
delicious [dɪ'lɪʃəs]	好吃的
pick	挑選
ripe [raɪp]	熟的
bin [bɪn]	貯藏箱
refrigerator [rɪ'frɪdʒəretɚ]	冰箱
spoil [spɔɪl]	壞了
squeeze [skwiz]	擠壓

Unit 3

At a Pharmacy
在藥房

◆ 對話一：依處方開藥

| 顧　客 | I'd like to have this prescription filled.
我想請你依這處方開藥。 |
| 藥劑師 | It'll only take a few minutes if you want to wait.
如果你要等的話，大概要幾分鐘。 |

（過一會兒……）

	Here you are. 好了，在這兒。
顧　客	Thank you. How often am I supposed to take it? 謝謝你，我多久要吃一次？
藥劑師	The instructions are written on the labels. 說明書在標籤上。

顧　客	Could you fill this prescription for me, please? 請你依這處方開藥給我，好嗎？
藥劑師	It will be ready in about 30 minutes. 大約30分鐘後會好。
顧　客	By the way, what do you suggest for insect bites? 還有，對於昆蟲咬，你有什麼藥嗎？
藥劑師	This ointment should help. 這個軟膏有效的。

◆ 對話三：買成藥

藥劑師	May I help you? 有什麼事嗎？
顧　客	Yes, I have an upset stomach. 是的，我的胃不舒服。
	Do you have any suggestion? 你有什麼藥嗎？
藥劑師	You don't have a prescription? 你沒有處方嗎？
顧　客	No. I sure don't. 沒有。

藥劑師	Well, our over-the-counter medicines for an upset stomach are on aisle 5. 那，我們治胃不舒服的成藥在第五排走道。
	There are many brands you may choose from. 有好幾個品牌你可以選。
顧　客	Thank you. 謝謝。

句型分析

→ 藥這個字，英文可以說drug or medicine.但drug又可指吃了會上癮的藥。因此，我們看到"Say no to drug"這個標語時，應知道，這裡的drug指的非法的毒品，而不是一般的成藥。一般的成藥，英文是over-the-counter medicine.（在櫃台買的藥）或non-prescription medicine（非處方的藥）。

→ 拿了處方，要請藥劑師開藥，用fill the prescription.

句型練習

請藥劑師依處方開藥

❖ I'd like to have this prescription filled.

　我想請你依這處方開藥。

❖ Could you fill this prescription for me, please?

可否請你依這處方開藥給我？

❖ I need to have this prescription filled.

我要你依這處方開藥。

吃藥

藥劑師	Here's some medicine for you to take. 這是你該吃的藥。
顧　客	How often am I supposed to take it? 我多久該吃一次？

請介紹成藥

顧　客	Have you got something for a rash? 你有沒有什麼藥可以治紅疹？
藥劑師	Try this cream. Many people say it works. 試試這個乳液，很多人都說有效。
顧　客	What do you suggest for dandruff? 對於頭皮屑你有沒有什麼辦法？
藥劑師	Try this shampoo. I think it'll help. 試試這種洗髮精，我想應該有幫助。

重要單字

pharmacist [ˈfɑrməsɪst]	藥劑師
prescription [prɪˈskrɪpʃən]	處方
prescription medicine [prɪˈskrɪpʃənˈmɛdɪʃən]	依處方開的藥
over-the-counter medicine [ˈovɚ ðə ˈkaʊntɚ]	成藥
drugstore	藥房
pharmacy [ˈfɑrməsɪ]	藥局
ointment [ˈɔɪntmənt]	軟膏
rash	紅疹
sunburn [ˈsʌnbɚn]	曬傷
chapped lips [tʃæpt ˈlɪps]	嘴唇裂
cough [kɔf]	咳嗽
headache [ˈhɛdˌek]	頭痛
a sore throat [ə sor ˈθrot]	喉嚨痛
an upset stomach [ən ˈʌpsɛt ˈstʌmək]	胃不舒服
insect bite [ˈɪnsɛkt baɪt]	昆蟲咬
dandruff [ˈdændrʌf]	頭皮屑

Around Town

在市區內

出國，除了到觀光點
遊覽之外，有些地方你還是
可能會去，例如：郵局、銀行、
美容院、理髮廳等。到不同的地
方，有不同地方需要的英語，
記住以下的句型，就可通行
無阻了。

Unit 1

Asking for Change
換零錢

◆ 對話一：要換零錢

旅 客	Excuse me, but do you have change for a dollar? 對不起，你有沒有零錢換這一塊錢。
外國人	I'll have to look. What do you want it for? 我要看看，你要做什麼用的？
旅 客	I want to make a phone call. 我要打電話。
外國人	You can use quarters, dimes and nickels. 你可以用25分硬幣，10分硬幣或是5分硬幣。

 句型分析

→ 要問別人事情，有打擾對方的意思，Excuse me.開頭，
再接下去問要問的事情。也可用Pardon me.兩者用法，
意思都一樣。

→ 問「為什麼」，本課用What?的句型，也可直接用Why?
因此本課的What do you need change for?也可說成
Why do you need change?

換零錢

❖ Do you have change for a dollar?

你有沒有零錢，換這一塊錢？

❖ Could you break a dollar?

你有沒有零錢，換這一塊錢？

❖ Could you give me change for a dollar?

你可以給我零錢換這一塊錢嗎？

❖ I can give you quarters, if that will help.

我可以給你25分錢的硬幣，如果那可以幫上忙的話。

❖ I need change for the parking meter.

我需要零錢投停車的碼錶。

❖ I think quarters will do.

我想25分硬幣應該可以用。

change	零錢
quarter ['kwɔrtɚ]	25分硬幣
dime [daɪm]	10分硬幣
nickel ['nɪkl̩]	5分硬幣
a dollar	一塊錢
break a dollar	把一塊錢換成零錢
parking meter ['pɑrkɪŋ 'mitɚ]	停車碼錶
stamp machine	售郵票機
vending machine ['vɛndɪŋ mə'ʃin]	自動販賣機
change machine	換零錢機

旅遊錦囊

　　美國的汽油分三種：Supreme（高級汽油）、plus（中級汽油）和regular（普通汽油）三種。不管你是自己加油，或是讓服務員幫你加，都得選擇一樣去加。

　　美國的加油站分：self-service（自助加油）和full-service（全套服務）兩種。全套服務，服務員不僅為你加油，還會幫你洗洗擋風玻璃等其他的服務。full-service的油每加侖比self-service的油貴。

Unit 2

In the Post Office
在郵局

Chapter 8

◆ 對話一：寄信

郵務員	Hello. Can I help you? 哈囉，有什麼事嗎？
旅　客	Yes, I need to send this letter to Taiwan. 是的，我要寄這封信到台灣。
郵務員	Airmail or surface mail? 航空還是水陸郵件。
旅　客	How much is an airmail letter to Taiwan? 到台灣的航空信多少？
郵務員	I'll have to check. Can I help you with anything else? 我要查一下，還有其他的事嗎？
旅　客	Yes, I'd like to buy five aerograms, please. 是的我要買五張郵簡。
郵務員	Here you go. 在這兒。

◆ 對話二：寄包裹

郵務員	Hello. May I help you? 哈囉，有什麼事？
旅 客	Hi. This package goes to Dallas, Texas. 嗨！這個包裹要寄到德州達拉斯。
郵務員	How do you want to send the package? First or fourth class? 你要如何寄？第一類，還是第四類？
旅 客	What's the difference between first and fourth class? 第一類和第四類有何不同？
郵務員	Fourth class mail is cheaper but slower. 第四類較便宜但較慢。
旅 客	Fourth class, please. 請用第四類。

◆ 對話三：美國國內掛號信

旅 客	To New York, please. 到紐約。
郵務員	Do you want the letter certified? 要掛號嗎？
旅 客	What does "certified" mean? 掛號是什麼意思？

郵務員	Certified mail is delivered with the regular mail. 掛號信與一般的郵件同時投遞。
	The person who receives it must sign for it. 收信人要簽收。

◆ 對話四：國際掛號信

旅　客	I'd like to send the letter by certified mail to Taiwan. 我要寄掛號信到台灣。
郵務員	No, you can't. There's no certified mail outside the U.S. 你不能寄，美國境外不能這麼寄。
旅　客	Well. What's the best way to send them? 那，我該怎麼寄呢？
郵務員	The best way is registered mail. 用國外掛號寄。

句型分析

→　不管是寄信、寄包裹、寄郵簡，都可用send這個字，
send～to某某地方，例如：Send this letter to Taiwan.
Send the parcel to New York.

→　講郵寄方式，用by這個介系詞，例如：by airmail（用航空寄），by registered mail（用掛號寄）。

→ 問對方要用什麼方式寄，用How這個字。例如：How do you want to send the letter?

→ 表達你想做什麼事，有三種句型可用：I need to～，I want to～或I'd like to～，to之後直接加上要做的事，原形動詞就可以。

句型練習

寄信

❖ I'd like to send this letter by airmail.

我想用航空寄這封信。

❖ I want to send the letter by certified mail.

我想用掛號寄這封信。

❖ I want to send the letter certified.

我要用掛號寄這封信。

❖ I'd like to send this letter registered to Tokyo.

我要用掛號寄這封信到東京。

寄包裹

❖ I need to send this parcel to Taiwan.

我要寄這包裹到台灣。

❖ I'd like to send this package by surface mail.

我用水陸寄這包裹。

❖ Send this package to New York, first class, please.

用第一類郵件寄這包裹到紐約。

❖ How do you want to send the package?

你要如何寄這包裹？

❖ Do you want the letter certified?

你這封信要掛號嗎？

❖ Do you want to send the letter certified?

你這封信要用掛號寄嗎？

 重要單字

airmail	航空郵件
surface mail ['sɜfɪs mel]	水陸郵件
registered mail ['rɛdʒɪstɚd]	郵簡
package ['pækɪdʒ]	包裹
parcel ['parsl̩]	包裹
first class	第一類郵件
fourth class	第四類郵件
post card	明信片

Chapter 8

Unit 3

At A Bank
在銀行

◆ 對話一：換現金

旅　客	I'd like to cash the travelers checks. 我要把這些旅行支票換成現金。
銀行員	May I see your photo ID? 可以給我看一看你有照片的證件嗎？
旅　客	How about my passport? 護照可以嗎？
銀行員	Yes, that will do. 是的，可以。
	How much do you want to cash? 你要換多少錢？
旅　客	Four hundred dollars. 四百元。
銀行員	How would you like them? 你要大鈔，還是小鈔？

旅　客	Twenties and some small bills, five's and one's. 二十元的，還有一些小鈔，例如五元的、一元的……

◆ 對話二：換現金

旅　客	I'd like to cash this $100.00 check. 我要換一百元現金。
銀行員	Sure. How do you want them? 好的，要大鈔，還是小鈔？
旅　客	Four twenties and two tens, please. 四張二十元的，二張十元的。

◆ 對話三：美金兌換台幣

旅　客	Would you tell me the current rate for NT dollars? 目前兌換台幣匯率是多少？
銀行員	One US dollar to 25 NT dollars. 一塊美金換二十五元台幣。
旅　客	Could you change the 5,000 NT dollars for me, please? 可否請你兌換這五千元台幣？
銀行員	Sure. 好的。

Chapter 8

旅　客	Excuse me. Can I buy a money order here? 對不起你們賣匯票嗎？
銀行員	One of the tellers can help you. 那些出納員中任何一個都可以。
旅　客	Where are they? 出納員在那裏？
銀行員	Next to new accounts. 在「開新戶頭」的旁邊。
	Just stand in the line over there. 你就排在那個隊伍就行了。
旅　客	Thank you. 謝謝。
銀行員	You're welcome. 不客氣。

句型分析

→ That will do.的do是「行」的意思。本句話的使用範圍很廣。凡是同意對方的提議，都可以說Okay, that will do.

→ 你要領現金時，有時職員會問你How do you want them?（你要大鈔還是小鈔？）你要用鈔票的單位來回答。如 "dollar bill", "ten's", "five's"等。

兌換現金

❖ Would you cash these travelers checks, please?

可否請你把這些旅行支票換成現金？

❖ How do you want them?

你要大鈔，還是小鈔？

❖ How would you like them?

你要大鈔，還是小鈔？

❖ Would you tell me the exchange rate?

你可否告訴我匯率是多少？

❖ I'd like to know the exchange rate for NT dollars.

我要知道換台幣的匯率是多少。

重要單字

ATM	自動提款機
money order	匯票
new account [njʊ əˈkaʊnt]	新帳戶
line	隊伍
travelers check [ˈtrævələ˞z tʃɛk]	旅行支票
exchange rate [ɪksˈtʃendʒ ret]	匯率
four twenties	四張二十元
two tens	二張十元

Unit 4

Getting a haircut
剪頭髮

◆ 對話一：剪頭髮

髮型師	What can I do for you today? 我能為你做什麼？
旅 客	I just want a trim. 我只要修剪一下。
髮型師	How would you like to have it cut? 要剪什麼樣子？
旅 客	Trim the back, but leave it long on the sides, please. 後面修剪一下，但兩邊還是留長。
髮型師	Do you want a shampoo? 要不要洗頭。
旅 客	Yes, please. 好的。

◆ 對話二：燙頭髮

旅　客	My hair looks so dull and flat. 我的頭髮看起來很塌又沒精神。
髮型師	I think you should get a perm. 我想你該燙一下。
旅　客	Do you have any suggestions in the hair style? 你能建議一下什麼髮型嗎？
髮型師	Let's look through these books. 我們來看看這些書。
	We may get some ideas. 可能會有些主意。

◆ 對話三：剪頭髮

髮型師	Do you need a haircut? 你要剪頭髮嗎？
旅　客	Yes. And I'd like a shave, too. 是的，還要刮鬍鬚。
髮型師	How would you like me to cut it? 你要剪什麼樣子？
旅　客	Cut it short all over. 全部把它剪短。

✈ want a little trim.若是要洗，也要吹乾，並做頭髮，就説 I'd like a shampoo, set and style.

句型練習

剪頭髮

❖ How would you like me to cut it?

你要剪什麼樣子？

❖ What do you want me to do?

你要我做什麼？

❖ How do you like to have it cut?

你要剪什麼樣子？

❖ What can I do for you?

我能為你做什麼？

如何剪

❖ I just want a little trim today.

我今天只要修剪一下。

❖ Just trim a little off the sides.

兩邊修剪一下。

❖ Cut it short all over.

全部剪短。

❖ Cut the sides short, but leave the front like it is.

旁邊剪短，前面留像原來的樣子。

洗頭，做頭髮

❖ I'd like a shampoo and a trim.

我要洗頭髮並剪一下。

❖ I want a shampoo, set and style.

我要洗頭，做頭髮。

❖ I'd like to get a perm in my hair.

我要燙頭髮。

 重要單字

trim [trɪm]	修剪
shampoo [ʃæmˈpu]	洗髮精
perm [pɝm]	燙頭髮
style	做髮型
shave [ʃev]	刮鬍鬚

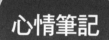

Making Phone Calls
打電話

到了美國機場，你很興奮想打電話給朋友，卻發現20元一張的旅行支票不能用來投幣，但你一定聽過有對方付費的電話吧？該如何讓接線生幫你撥呢？詳細練習本章各節，你就可以應付自如了。

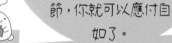

Unit 1

Personal Call
私人電話

◆ 對話一：接電話

外國人	Hello? 哈囉？
旅　客	Hello, is Jane there? 哈囉，珍在嗎？
外國人	This is Jane. 我就是珍。
旅　客	Hi, Jane. This is John. 嗨，珍，我是約翰。
外國人	Hi, John. How are you? 嗨，約翰，你好嗎？

◆ 對話二：是誰打電話來？

朋　友	Hello, this is the Wang residence. 哈囉，這裏是姓王。

旅　客	May I speak to Mary? 我可以跟瑪麗說話嗎？
朋　友	Who's calling, please? 請問你是誰？
旅　客	This is John Lee. I'm her friend from Taiwan. 我是李約翰，我是她從台灣來的朋友。
朋　友	Just a minute, please. 請等一下。

對話三：要找的人不在

外國人	Hello. 哈囉。
旅　客	May I speak to Linda? 我可以跟玲達說話嗎？
外國人	Linda is not in right now. May I take a message? 玲達不在，要留話嗎？
旅　客	No, thanks. I'll call back later. 不用了，謝謝，我以後再打來。

對話四：要留話嗎？

外國人	He is not in. May I take a message? 他不在，要留話嗎？

旅　客	Could you tell him to give John a call? 你可以請他打電話給約翰嗎？
	He has my number. 他有我的電話。
外國人	O.K. I'll be glad to tell him that. 好的，我很樂意告訴他。

句型分析

→ 有人打電話來，對方要找的人不在，我們大都會順便問
對方May I take a message?（要留話嗎？）

→ 有人打電話來，你接了電話，對方正好要找你，你可以
説This is he speaking.或者簡單地説，Speaking.

→ 在電話中問對方，"你是誰？"要説"Who is this?" 不要説
"Who are you?"

句型練習

要請某人聽電話

❖ May I speak to Mr. Lin?

我可以跟林先生講電話嗎？

❖ Is Tom in?

湯姆在嗎？

❖ Is John there?

約翰在嗎？

❖ Jenny Lin, please.

請林珍妮聽電話。

接到電話的稱呼

❖ Speaking.

我就是。

❖ This is he.

我就是。

❖ This is she.

我就是。

❖ Who's calling, please?

請問你是誰？

❖ Who's this, please?

請問你是誰？

稍候

❖ Hold on, please.

請稍候。

❖ Hang on, please.

請稍候。

❖ Just a minute, please.
請等一下。

❖ Just a moment, please.
請等一下。

❖ Hang on a minute.
等一下。

❖ He's on another line. Can you hold?
他在講另一個電話，你要等嗎？

欲找對象不在

❖ He is not in. May I take a message?
他不在，你要留話嗎？

❖ He is out for shopping. He'll be back soon. Would you call back in ten minutes?
他出去購物，很快就回來，你再過十分鐘再打好嗎？

❖ She is not here right now. She's at work.
她不在，她在上班。

待會兒再打

❖ I'll call her back later.
我待會兒再打給她。

❖ Do you know when he'll be back?
你知不知道他什麼時候回來？

留言

❖ Would you please tell her Jenny called?

可否請你告訴她珍妮打電話找她？

❖ Would you please ask her to call Tom at 211-1234?

可否請你要她打電話給211-1234找湯姆。

❖ Could you tell her to give John a call? She has my number.

可否請你要她打電話給約翰，她有我的電話號碼。

傳話

❖ I'll tell her as soon as she gets home.

她一回來我馬上告訴她。

❖ O.K. I'll be glad to tell her that.

好的，我很樂意告訴她。

❖ I'll make sure she gets the message.

我一定把話傳到。

重要單字

residence ['rɛzɪdəns]	住宅
message ['mɛsɪdʒ]	留話

Unit 2

Wrong Number
打錯電話

◆ 對話一：打錯電話

外國人	Hello? 哈囉？	
旅　客	Is Mary there? 瑪麗在嗎？	
外國人	I'm sorry. You have the wrong number. 對不起，你打錯電話了。	
旅　客	Oh, is this 211-1234? 噢，這裡是211-1234嗎？	
外國人	No, it's not. 不是。	
旅　客	I'm sorry. 對不起。	
外國人	That's O.K. 沒關係。	

外國人	Hello? 哈囉？
旅　客	May I speak to Mr. Lee? 我可以跟李先生說話嗎？
外國人	You have the wrong number. 你打錯電話了。
旅　客	I do? 是嗎？
外國人	What number did you dial? 你要撥幾號？
旅　客	211-2348. 211-2348。
外國人	This is 2347. 這裏是2347。
旅　客	I'm sorry to have bothered you. 很抱歉打擾你了。
外國人	That's O.K. 沒關係。

Chapter 9

外國人	Hello? 哈囉？
旅　客	Is Jane in? 珍在嗎？
外國人	Whom do you want to talk to? 你要跟誰說話？
旅　客	Jane Lee. 李珍。
外國人	There is no one here by that name. 這裏沒有人叫這個名字。
旅　客	Is this 344-1288? 這裏是344-1288嗎？
外國人	Yes, but there isn't anyone called Jane here. 是的，但這裏沒有人叫珍。
旅　客	Oh, I'm sorry. 噢，對不起。

句型分析

✈ 問對方想跟誰說話，Whom do you want to talk to?跟
誰說話的誰是當talk to的受詞，用疑問詞Who的受格
Whom比較正式,口語上用who也可以。跟誰說話是talk

to，記住to不能省略。

→ 人家告訴你，你打錯電話了，你半信半疑，問"是嗎？"英文說I do?把句尾語調提高，（注意聽MP3）。千萬不要拘泥於舊文法，說成"Do I?"

告訴對方，他打錯電話了

❖ Wrong number.

你打錯電話了。

❖ You have the wrong number.

你打錯電話了。

❖ I'm afraid you have the wrong number.

我恐怕你是打錯電話了。

❖ There is no one here by that name.

這裡沒有人叫那個名字。

確認電話號碼

❖ Is this 211-1234?

這裡是211-1234嗎？

❖ Is this City Bank?

這裡是花旗銀行嗎？

道歉撥錯電話I

❖ I'm sorry.

　對不起。

❖ I'm sorry to have bothered you.

　對不起，打擾了。

重要單字

dial [daɪl]	撥（電話）
bother [ˈbɑðə]	（打擾）

Unit 3

Through the Operator
經由接線生

◆ 對話一：打對方付費電話

接線生	This is the Operator. May I help you? 這裡是接線生，有什麼事嗎？
旅　客	I'd like to make a collect call to Dallas, Texas. The area code is 214. The number is 432-8177. 我要打對方付費的電話到德州，達拉斯。區域號碼是214，號碼是432-8177。
接線生	What is your name? 你叫什麼名字？
旅　客	Bob Lee. 李保勃。

（接線生接通後，先與對方說話）

外國人	Hello. 哈囉？

接線生	You have a collect call from Bob Lee, at Los Angeles. Will you accept the charges? 你有一通從洛杉磯李保勃打的，由你付費的電話你要付錢嗎？
外國人	O.K. 好的。

（接線生對李保勃說話）

接線生	Go ahead, please. 請開始通話。

◆ 對話二：查號台

接線生	Directory Assistance. May I help you? 查號台，有什麼事嗎？
旅　客	Yes, I'd like the number of Mary Chen, please. C-H-E-N, Chen. 有，請給我陳瑪麗的電話……拼做CHEN.。
接線生	The number is 211-1234. 電話是211-1234。
旅　客	Thank you. 謝謝你。

→ I'd like～（我想要）這個句型。很常用，是I would like～的縮寫。如果加名詞的話，就直接加上去，例如：I'd like a coke.（我要一杯可樂）。如果後面加動詞的話，要先加to再加動詞，I'd like to make a collect call.

句型練習

指示接線生

❖ I'd like to place a person-to-person call.

我要打叫人電話。

❖ I'd like to place a station-to-station call.

我要打叫號電話。

❖ I'd like to place a long-distance call.

我要打長途電話。

❖ I'd like to make an overseas call.

我要打國際電話。

❖ I'd like to make a collect call.

我要打對方付費電話。

Chapter 9

❖ The line is busy.

對方電話方中。

❖ Go ahead, please.

請通話。

❖ No one answers the phone.

沒有人接電話。

❖ Shall I keep trying and let you know when I get through?

你要我繼續打，等打通了再告訴你嗎？

重要單字

area code [ˈɛrɪə kod]	區域號碼
operator [ˈɑpəˌretɚ]	接線生
long distance call	長途電話
person-to-person call	叫人電話
station-to-station call	叫號電話
collect call [kəˈlɛkt kɔl]	對方付費電話
directory assistance [dəˈrɛktərɪ əˈsɪstəns]	查號台

Business Call
商業電話

◆ 對話一：打到公司找人

祕 書	Peter Wang's office. May I help you? 這裏是王彼德的辦公室，有什麼事嗎？
旅 客	May I speak to Mr. Wang? 我可以跟王先生講話嗎？
祕 書	He's at a meeting. 他在開會。
	May I take a message? 你要留話嗎？
旅 客	No, thank you. I'll call back later. 不，謝謝，我以後再打。

◆ 對話二： 請人轉分機

| 總 機 | Pacific Company, this is Nancy.
太平洋公司，我是南茜。 |

	May I help you? 有什麼事嗎？
旅　客	Extension 209, please. 請轉209分機。

◆ 對話三：問打電話的人是誰

總　機	May I tell Mr. Lin who's calling? 我可以告訴林先生是誰打來的嗎？
旅　客	Certainly. This is Mary Lee with ABC International company. 可以，我是ABC國際公司的林瑪麗。

句型分析

→ May I tell～who's calling?的句型是用來問對方是誰，在
　非商業場合，可以說Who is this?但商務上絕對要用本
　句型或May I ask who's this?（可以請問您是那裡嗎？）

→ 電話中說我是某某人，英文是This is某某人，而不是I
　am某某人。

→ 打電話到某個公司，接電話者通常會自報公司的名字，
　和自己的名字。接電話者若是某人的祕書，會說這裡是
　某某人的辦公室。

句型練習

在上班地點接到電話

❖ Lucky Travel. May I help you?

　幸福旅行社，有什麼事嗎？

❖ John Lee's office. May I help you?

　李約翰的辦公室，有什麼事嗎？

某人不在

❖ He's away from his desk.

　他剛離開。

❖ He just stepped out.

　他剛出去。

❖ He's at a meeting.

　他在開會。

❖ He is talking to a customer right now.

　他正在與一位客人說話。

❖ He is busy now.

　他現在很忙。

❖ He is not available now.

　他現在不能接電話。

❖ He'll be back in an hour.

他一小時後會回來。

❖ He won't be back this afternoon.

他今天下午不會再回辦公室了。

❖ He won't be back until 2 o'clock this afternoon.

他今天下午二點才會回來。

傳話

❖ I'll have him call you back.

我會請他回你電話。

❖ I'll be sure he gets the message.

我一定會把話傳給他。

再打給你

❖ I'm on another line. May I call you later?

我正在講另一個電話，我再打給你好嗎？

❖ I'll call you back in 30 minutes.

我三十分鐘後再打給你。

telephone directory	電話號碼簿
white page	不分類商業、住宅電話號碼簿
yellow page	分類電話號碼簿
overseas call ［'ovɚsiz kɔl］	國際電話
extension [ɪks'tɛnʃən]	分機
charge	收費
hang up	掛斷電話
pay phone	公用電話
public phone ['pʌblɪk fon]	公用電話
private phone ['praɪvɪt]	自用電話
line	電話線
busy	佔線

旅遊錦囊

當你打collect call時，對方聽到接線生告訴他的第一句話就是Will you pay for the charges?所以，當你到美國機場，興沖沖地想打collect call時可要三思了。

在對美國打電話，若要找接線生幫忙，可撥"0"，就可與接線生講話。

美國的查號台號碼是1411。

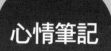

Chapter 10

At the Gas Station
在加油站

在美國加油，
大部分是自助式加油。
也可以讓服務人員幫你加油，
你可知道要把油加滿怎麼説？

Self-Serve
自助加油

◆ 對話一：學自己加油

外國人	You want to fill it up, don't you? 你要加滿，是不是？
旅　客	Yes, but do you know how to pump gas? 是的，但是你知道如何加油嗎？
外國人	No, but I'll try. 不知道，但我想試試看。
旅　客	O.K. Go ahead. 好的，你加吧。
外國人	Look, the lever lets up. It's done, isn't it? 你看，槓桿彈起來了加好了，是嗎？
旅　客	Yes. Let's pay and get going. 是的，我們付了錢，就走。

→ 打氣的英文是pump air，加油是pump gas。把油加滿是fill up the gas tank，輪胎沒氣了，是flat tire.

→ 本對話用到兩個附加問句～，don't you?和～，isn't it? 到底要用前者還是後者要看句子本身的動詞來決定。對話第一句的動詞是want（要），屬普通動詞，所以附加問句用do來取代want。同時，附加問句的語氣要與原句子相反，所以肯定句要加否定附加問句，於是產生了don't you?的附加問句。對話的第五句。因為It's done. 的動詞是is，屬Be動詞附加問句也用Be動詞is的否定isn't it就可以了。

打氣

❖ Do you know how to pump air?

你知道如何打氣嗎？

❖ Check the tires and pump air, if necessary.

檢查一下輪胎，如有需要，就打氣。

❖ We'll stop at the gas station to fill up the gas tank and pump air.

我們要在加油站停，加滿油，並打氣。

加油

❖ Do you know how to pump gas?

你知道如何加油嗎？

❖ Let's stop for gas.

我們停下來加油。

❖ Let's stop for gas and check the tires.

我們停下來加油，打氣。

❖ Take off the gas cap.

把油箱蓋子拿掉。

❖ Flip the lever to the ON position.

把槓桿轉到「開」的位置上。

❖ Put the nozzle in the gas tank.

把加油管口放進油箱。

❖ When the tank is full, the lever lets up.

油箱滿時，槓桿會彈起來。

 重要單字

pump gas [pʌmp gæs]	加油
self-serve	自助加油
lever [ˈlɛvɚ]	槓桿
flip [flɪp]	轉
nozzle [ˈnɑzl̩]	加油管口

Unit 2

Full-Serve
全套服務

◆ 對話一：把油加滿

旅　客	Fill it up with Supreme, please. 加滿九三高級汽油。
加油工	Sure. Do you want your windshield cleaned? 好的，要洗一下擋風玻璃嗎？
旅　客	No, thank you. I don't have time. 不用了，謝謝，我沒有時間。
	How much is it? 一共多少錢？
加油工	It comes to $15.00. 一共是十五元。

◆ 對話二：要換機油

加油工	Hello, what can I do for you today? 哈囉，今天有什麼事嗎？

Chapter 10

165

旅　客	Fill it up with Unleaded Plus, please. 請加滿中級無鉛汽油。
加油工	Certainly. 好的。
旅　客	By the way, it's about time to change the oil. 還有，我該換機油了。
	I don't have time today. 今天沒時間。
	May I stop by some other time and have it done? 我改天過來換機油好嗎？
加油工	Sure. How about Friday afternoon? 好的，星期五下午好嗎？
旅　客	That's fine. See you then. 好，再見。

句型分析

→ 加油時要注意「油」的說法。oil是指機油，gas是指汽油。說錯了就麻煩了！

→ 有些句型，可用主動，也可以用被動，所表達的意思是一樣的。例如說，要檢查機油，可以說Should I check your oil?這裡用人去檢查機油，所以，用主動的說法。同樣這句話，也可以說Do you want your oil checked. 指機油被檢查，用被動的說法。

→ Supreme，Unleaded Plus首字母雖然用大寫，但不是專有名詞，只是在句子裡強調是油品的等級而已。美國各石油公司的汽油分級用字略有不同，但加油工一定聽得懂這兩個字。

把油加滿

❖ Fill it up, please.
請把油加滿。

❖ Fill it up with regular.
加滿普通汽油。

其他服務

❖ Should I check your tires?
你要我檢查輪胎嗎？

❖ Should I clean your windshield?
你要我洗擋風玻璃嗎？

❖ Do you want your tires checked?
你要我檢查輪胎嗎？

❖ Do you want your windshield cleaned?
你要我洗一下擋風玻璃嗎？

❖ Do you want me to check the oil?

你要我檢查機油嗎？

❖ Do you want me to take a look at the tires?

你要我檢查一下輪胎嗎？

請做以下的服務

❖ Would you check the lights, please?

請檢查一下燈，好嗎？

❖ Could you clean the rear window, too?

也請洗一下後面的窗戶，好嗎？

❖ Check the oil, too.

也檢查一下機油。

 重要單字

spare tire [spɛr taɪr]	備胎
flat tire [flæt]	爆胎
check the oil	檢查機油
fill it up	把油箱加滿
gas tank	油箱
windshield [ˈwɪndʃɪld]	擋風玻璃
full-service [ˈfʊl sɜ˞vɪs]	全套服務
gas	汽油

supreme [sjʊˈprim]	高級汽油
plus [plʌs]	中級汽油
regular [ˈrɛgjʊlɚ]	普通汽油
unleaded [ʌnˈlɛdɪd]	無鉛汽油
gas cap	油箱蓋子
pump	加（油）；打（油）
check	檢查
brake [brek]	剎車

旅遊錦囊

　　對於別人說的話，一時沒聽清楚，請對方再說一遍，只要說得得體，對方一定會樂意再重說一次的。

　　向別人提出要求時，也一樣要盡量用客氣的語氣，例如：Would you mind if～?或是I was wondering if～?等，如此，對方才會樂意答應你的請求，注意if後面的動詞可以用過去式，整個語氣更客氣一些。

Chapter 11

Transportation
交通

出外旅行，不外乎
自己開車、搭計程車、
坐公車或坐火車，每一個單
元的情況對話，都是你到
國外旅行，最基本的英
語，不可不會。

Unit 1

On the Road
開車上路旅行

MP3-31

◆ 對話一：在路上

太太	We've driven all day now. 我們已經開了一天了。
先生	Right! We still have a long way to go, though. 是啊！還有一段路要開呢！
太太	How about staying at a hotel in a city tonight? 今晚在城裏找個旅館過夜好嗎？
先生	All right. I'll check the map to see which city we are near. 好的，我查一下地圖看我們靠近那個城市。

◆ 對話二：休息區

太太	How far have we been on Interstate 90? 我們在九十號州際公路上開多遠了？

172

先 生	About ten miles. We're going to take the Highway 14 exit. 大約十里了，我們要從高速公路十四號出去。
太 太	Would you stop at the next rest area? 你在下一個休息區停一下好嗎？
	The kids are getting hungry and I need to stretch my legs. 小孩子肚子餓了，我也需要伸伸腿。
先 生	Sure thing. 好的。

句型分析

✈ 問別人要不要做某事用How about～? How about後面要加動名詞，例如：How about drinking some water? （喝點水吧！）

✈ 請別人做某某事，用Would you～?或Would you please～?後面加原形動詞，例如：Would you try to find a motel?（可不可以請你找一間汽車旅館？）

✈ Way在本課指距離，例：It is a long way to Beijing.（到北京距離很遠）。

停車休息

❖ Let's stop soon. We've driven enough for one day.

　我們儘快停一下。我們這樣一天下來開得夠久了。

❖ We've driven all day now.

　我們已經開了一整天了。

❖ Would you stop at the next rest area?

　你在下一個休息區停一下好嗎？

查看地圖

❖ I'll look at the map to see exactly where we are.

　我要看地圖，看我們確實在那裏。

❖ I 'll check the map to see which city we are near.

　我要看地圖，看我們靠近那個城市。

注意出口

❖ We have to watch for Exit 18.

　我們必須注意十八號出口。

❖ We have to watch for San Diego Freeway.

　我們必須注意聖地牙哥公路。

❖ We're taking the next exit.

我們下個出口要出去。

❖ We still have two more exits to go.

我們還有兩個出口就要出去。

❖ The exit we're taking is two miles away.

我們要出去的出口還有兩哩。

重要單字

interstate highway [ˈɪntəˌstet ˈhaɪwe]	州際高速公路
highway	高速公路
freeway [ˈfriwe]	高速公路
tollway [ˈtolwe]	收費公路
exit [ˈɛgzɪt]	出口
rest area [rɛst ˈɛrɪə]	休息區
ramp [ræmp]	交流道
drive	開
go	走
stretch [strɛtʃ]	伸長
exactly	正好
city	城市
map	地圖
mile	哩
near	靠近

Unit 2

At a Bus Station
在公車站

◆ 對話一：閒聊

旅　客	Hi. Are you waiting for a bus? 嗨，你在等公車嗎？
外國人	Yes. 是的。
旅　客	When does your bus leave? 你的公車什麼時候開？
外國人	It leaves at five o'clock. 在五點開。
	When does your bus leave? 你的幾點開？
旅　客	Five-thirty. Where are you going? 五點三十分，你要去那裏？
外國人	I'm going to Boston. 我要去波士頓。

◀ 對話二：搭公車

旅　客　Which bus do we take to the Performing Art Center?
要去文藝中心該搭那班公車？

外國人　Bus #208.
208號公車。

We get off at Main street and 11th, and walk down Main street.
我們在緬因街和11街下車，沿著緬因街走下去。

◀ 對話三：搭灰狗巴士

旅　客　I'm taking Greyhound bus to Chicago.
我要搭灰狗巴士去芝加哥。

外國人　That's a long trip.
那是長途旅行。

旅　客　Yes, it is.
是的。

It'll take a full day to get there.
要一整天才到那兒。

But it would be a great experience.
但是，那會是一次很好的經驗。

旅　客	How much is a bus ticket to Chicago? 到芝加哥的票價多少？
售票員	One way or round trip? 單程或來回？
旅　客	Would you quote me for both, please? 兩樣都告訴我價錢好嗎？
售票員	Sure. One way is $36.00. Round trip is $70.00. 好的，單程是36元，來回是70元。
旅　客	What time does it leave? 何時離開。
售票員	At 7:15 p.m. 下午7點15分。
旅　客	I'd like two one-way tickets, please. 我喜歡兩張單程車票。

◆ 對話五：買車票

旅　客	I'd like a round-trip tickets to San Francisco, please. 我要一張到舊金山的來回票。

售票員	O.K. That's $23.55. 好的,那是23元55分。
旅　客	May I write a personal check? 我寫一張私人支票給你好嗎?
售票員	That's fine. We accept personal checks. 沒問題,我們收私人支票。
旅　客	When does the bus get there? 公車何時到那裏?
售票員	It arrives in San Francisco at 5:30 p.m. 在下午5點半到舊金山。

◆ 對話六:到市中心

旅　客	I want to go downtown. 我要去市中心。
	Which bus should I take? 我該搭那班公車?
外國人	Take the #201 bus. 搭201號公車。
	It leaves every 20 minutes. 每20分一班。

句型分析

→ I'm taking Greyhound bus to Chicago.（我正要搭灰狗巴士去芝加哥），是用現在進行式表示即將發生的事情。若是天天發生的事，用現在式就可以，例如：I take the bus to work.（我每天搭公車上班）。

句型練習

車費是多少？

❖ How much is a round-trip ticket?

來回票票價多少？

❖ How much is a one-way ticket?

單程票票價多少？

❖ How much is the fare?

車費是多少？

搭公車

❖ Where can I catch a bus?

我在那裏搭公車？

❖ Did they change the bus schedule?

他們改了公車時間表嗎？

❖ There's a bus stop on the corner.

角落處有個公車站。

❖ I go to work by bus.

我搭公車上班。

 重要單字

bus stop	公車招呼
bus station [bʌs ˈsteʃən]	公車站
Greyhound [ˈgreˌhaʊnd]	灰狗巴士
trip	旅行
experience [ɪkˈspɪrɪəns]	經驗
ticket	車票
one way ticket	單程車票
round trip ticket	來回車票
quote [kwot]	報價
arrive	到達
downtown [ˈdaʊntaʊn]	市中心
schedule [ˈskɛdʒʊl]	時刻表
corner [ˈkɔrnɚ]	角落

Taking a Taxi

搭計程車

◆ 對話一：打電話叫車

旅　　客	Could you please send a taxi to the Hilton Hotel downtown? 你可以派一輛計程車到市中心的希爾頓飯店嗎？
車　　行	Sure. When do you want it? 好的，你什麼時候要？
旅　　客	As soon as possible. 越快越好。
車　　行	There'll be a cab there in about twenty minutes. 20分鐘內會有一輛計程車到。

◆ 對話二：打電話叫車

旅　　客	I need a taxi. 我需要一輛計程車。

車　行	Where are you? 你在那裏？
旅　客	I'm at the Holiday Inn on Airport Boulevard. 我在機場大道的假日旅館。
車　行	O.K. I'll send one. 好的，我會派一輛過去。
旅　客	How soon will it be here? 多久會到？
車　行	In about fifteen minutes. 大約要15分。

◆ 對話三：在路邊叫計程車

旅　客	Taxi. 計程車。

（車子停下）

	I want to go to the Empire State Building. 我要去帝國大廈。
司　機	Sure thing. 好的。
旅　客	About how much will the fare be? 車費大約多少？

Chapter 11

司　機	I think that'll be around $20.00. 我想大約要20美元。

◆ 對話四：搭計程車

旅　客	Kennedy Airport, please. I have to be there by 7：00. 到甘迺迪機場，我7點一定要到。
司　機	We shouldn't have any trouble if the traffic isn't too heavy. 如果交通不太擁擠的路，應該沒問題。

（到了機場）

司　機	Here we are. $12.50, please. 到了，是12塊半。
旅　客	Thank you. Here's $13.00. 謝謝，這兒有13元。
	Keep the change. 不用找了。

句型分析

→ 搭計程車，常遇見交通擁擠，或是一路遇到紅燈。交通
很擠的説法是The traffic is heavy.遇到很多紅燈的説法
是hit many red lights.

→ change當動詞是改變的意思，當名詞是零錢，給錢時，
若要付小費，可以叫對方不用找了，通常都是説keep
the change,也就是把零錢收著。

句型練習

交通阻塞

❖ We got stuck in a traffic jam.

我們被困在交通阻塞中。

❖ We got held up in traffic.

我們被困在交通阻塞中。

❖ We got caught in rush-hour traffic.

我們被困在尖峰時間的交通阻塞中。

紅燈

❖ The lights are with us.

我們都沒遇到紅燈。

❖ We didn't hit many red lights.

我們都沒遇到紅燈。

重要單字

airport	機場
trouble ['trʌbḷ]	麻煩
change	零錢
lights	燈
heavy traffic	交通很擁擠
rush-hour ['rʌʃ aʊr]	尖峰時間
traffic jam ['træfɪk dʒæm]	塞車
traffic	交通
taxi	計程車

Unit 4

At a Railroad Station
在火車站

◆ 對話一：搭火車

旅　客	What time does the train for Washington leave? 到華盛頓的火車幾點開？
服務員	8:30 on Track 5. 8點30分在5號鐵軌。
旅　客	When does it arrive? 何時到？
服務員	It should be there at 10:30, but it may be a little late. 應該10點半會到，但可能會遲一些。
旅　客	What's the round-trip fare? 來回票是多少？
服務員	It's $52.00. 52元。

◆ 對話二：搭火車

旅　客	Which train do I take to Chicago? 去芝加哥我要搭那班火車？
服務員	That's platform 3 at 10:30. 10點半在3號月台那班。
旅　客	When does it get there? 何時到那裏？
服務員	It's scheduled to arrive at 12:45. 應該是12點45分會到。

◆ 對話三：問火車票價

旅　客	How much is a ticket to Washington, D.C.? 到華盛頓特區的票價是多少？
售票員	Would it be one-way or round-trip? 是單程還是來回。
旅　客	One way, please. 單程。
售票員	It's $15.00 one way. 單程是15元。

句型分析

→ 單程是做名詞，英文是one way.若是用做形容詞，是 one-way.

→ 問車費多少？可説What's the fare?或是How much is a ticket?

→ 火車由那裏開？英語都是用幾號軌道，例如火車在8點 30分，由Track 5開。但國內都説月台，所以用platform 5也可以。

句型練習

問時間

❖ What time does the train for Baltimore leave?

到巴爾的摩的火車何時開？

❖ When does the train get to Atlanta?

這班火車幾點到亞特蘭大？

問那班火車

❖ Is this the train for San Francisco?

這是到舊金山的火車嗎？

❖ Does the train go to New Jersey?

這班火車到紐澤西州嗎？

❖ Which train do I take to Philadelphia?

到費城要搭那班火車？

問月台

❖ What track does the train leave from?

這班火車從幾號軌離開？

❖ What platform does the train leave from?

這班火車從幾號月台離開？

問時間

❖ What time is the next train to Washington?

到華盛頓的下一班火車是幾點？

❖ What time does the train for Boston leave?

到波士頓的火車幾點離開？

問票價

❖ How much is a one-way ticket?

單程車票是多少錢？

❖ What's the round-trip fare?

來回票是是多少錢？

❖ What's the fare?

車資是多少？

❖ It's $30.00 one way or $55.00 round trip.

單程是30元，來回是55元。

重要單字

track 5 [træk]	5號軌道
platform [ˈplætfɔrm]	月台
fare [fɛr]	車資
round-trip fare	來回票價

旅遊錦囊

　　美國的州際高速公路都有編號。

偶數號碼指東西向的高速公路。奇數號碼指

南北向。所以，你若聽到有人開在十號高速公

路。你可以想像，此人或是向東往佛羅里達州的方

向，或是向西往加州的方向開。

　　美國有些城市的計程車並不滿街跑，到處找客

人。所以，要搭計程車需先打電話到車行叫車。

　　美國的里程數是以mile（哩）來計算，10哩約等

於16公里。

　　美國高速公路限速在近都市是55 mile（90公

里），市外是65 mile（105公里）。但經過市區

時，則各市限制不同所以進入市區，不管都

市大小，都要注意速限標誌。

Chapter 11

Chapter 12

General Conversation
各種場合會話

到國外旅行，除了
學一些情況英語以外，
一般 的會話，如請對方
再重説一遍，要求別人幫
忙等也要知道怎麼説。

Unit 1

Asking People to Repeat
要求對方再重說一遍

◆ 對話一：請再說一遍

外國人	Do you need any help? 需要幫忙嗎？
旅　客	I beg your pardon? 請再說一遍。
外國人	I asked if you needed any help. 我問你是否需要幫忙？
旅　客	Yes. If it's not too much trouble, I would like some help. 是的。如果不會太麻煩的話，我需要你的幫忙。
外國人	It's no trouble at all. 一點也不麻煩。

194

旅 客	I'm sorry, but I didn't catch what you said. 對不起，但我沒聽清楚你說的話。
外國人	I said, "Is there anything I can do?". 我說：「需要我幫忙嗎？」
旅 客	If you wouldn't mind, I could use some help. 如果你不介意的話，請幫一下忙。
外國人	Just tell me what you'd like me to do. 只要告訴我，你要我做什麼就好了。

句型分析

→ 間接問句是把疑問句拿來做受詞，問句的句型要改變。
例如，疑問句Do you need any help?改成間接問句時，
先用if（是否）再看新句子的動詞，因為這裡asked是過
去式，所以need也改成過去式，句型變成I asked if you
needed any help.

→ 請對方把剛說的話，重說一次，除了用I beg your
pardon?外，也可用Pardon me?注意這兩句的句尾語調
都必須提高。

句型練習

請再重說一次

❖ Sorry, but I didn't catch what you said.

對不起，沒聽清楚你說什麼？

❖ I didn't quite hear what you said.

我沒聽清楚你說什麼？

❖ I beg your pardon?

請再重說一遍？

提議幫忙

❖ Is there anything I can do?

我能為你做什麼？

❖ Do you need any help?

你需要幫忙嗎？

❖ Do you want a ride?

你需要我載你嗎？

重覆剛說過的話

❖ I asked if there was anything I could do.

我剛說我能為你做什麼。

❖ I asked if you needed any help.

我剛剛問你是否需要幫忙。

❖ I asked if you wanted a ride.

我剛剛問你是否需要我載你。

 重要單字

ride	用車子載
quite	相當
trouble	麻煩
catch	趕上

Unit 2

Asking Favors
提出要求

◆ 對話一：借車

外國人	Would you mind if I borrow your car? 你介意我借你的車子嗎？
旅　客	Yes, I do. Last time you borrowed my car and returned it with an empty gas tank. 是的，我介意，上回你借我的車，還給我車時油缸都沒油了。
外國人	Oh, I'm sorry. I promise you this time I'll fill it up. 對不起，我向你保證，這次一定會把油缸加滿。
旅　客	No. I don't trust you any more. 不，我不再信任你了。

◆ 對話二：借打字機

旅　客	I wonder if I may borrow your typewriter. 我不知道可不可以借你的打字機。

外國人	It really depends on when you need it. 那要看你是什麼時候要借。
旅　客	This weekend. 這個週末。
外國人	I have a report due next Monday. 下星期一，我有個報告要交。
	I need my typewriter this weekend, too. 這個週末我也需要用打字機。

→ 有人用Would you mind～向你提出要求時，你若是不想答應，要說Yes, I do.（是的，我介意），表示拒絕對方的要求。如果，你要答應對方的要求就說，**No, I don't**（不，我不介意），表示答應對方的要求。

提出要求

❖ May I borrow your typewriter?

我可以向你借打字機嗎？

❖ Can I have a cup of coffee?

我可以要一杯咖啡嗎？

❖ I was wondering if I could borrow your car.

我不知道是否可以借你的車子。

❖ Do you think I could bring Sally to your party?

我可以帶莎利來參加你的宴會嗎？

❖ Can you do some shopping for me?

你可以去替我買些東西嗎？

❖ Can you show me how to get there?

你可以告訴我如何去那兒嗎？

答應對方

❖ Would you mind if I turned on the TV?

我打開電視的話，你會介意嗎？

❖ No, go right ahead.

不會，儘管開。

 重要單字

typewriter [ˈtaɪpraɪtɚ]	打字機
mind	介意
turn on	打開
borrow	借
exactly	正好
holiday	假期

guess	猜
wonder	奇怪
depend on	依～而定

旅遊錦囊

在美國，不管是打電話，或是投幣機，都可用25分、10分或是5分的硬幣，但penny（1分的硬幣）卻不行。

旅行支票（travelers check）在美國可以當現金用，不一定非到銀行去兌換現金不可。但，收銀員大都會要求看有照片的證件。當然，你的護照是絕對可以用。但有時，你不巧沒帶護照，或是遇到少見多怪的收銀員，她還要去請示經理，浪費你的時間。為了省麻煩，到銀行把旅行支票換成現金好了。

美國國內的掛號信叫certified mail.寄到美國國外的掛號信叫 registered mail.。在美國國內寄普通郵件，可用第一類或第四類郵件，第四類郵件較便宜但較慢。

Unit 3

The Weather
天氣

◆ 對話一：談天氣

旅　客	I think it's going to be a nice day. 我想今天應該會是好天氣。
外國人	Yes, the weather forecast said it would be sunny and warm. 是啊！氣象預報說，今天應該會是晴天，而且很溫暖。
旅　客	I just hope it doesn't get cold again. 我只是希望別再冷了。
外國人	It's spring. I don't think it'll be too cold. 已經是春天了，應該不會太冷了。

◆ 對話二：下大雨

| 旅　客 | Is it raining now?
外面在下雨嗎？ |
| 外國人 | Yes, it's raining cats and dogs.
是啊，下得很大。 |

旅 客	Oh, what am I going to do? 噢，我該怎麼辦？
	I didn't bring an umbrella. 我沒帶雨。
外國人	Don't worry. It should stop soon. 沒擔心，很快就會停的。

句型分析

→ It's raining cats and dogs.是說雨下得很大。或是說正下著傾盆大雨。這是一句很常見的成語，記住這句成語，遇到下大雨時可以用。你的美國朋友一定會覺得你的英語很好。

句型練習

談天氣

❖ It's supposed to get colder today.

今天應該會冷些。

❖ It looks like it's going to be a nice day.

看起來，今天天氣會很好。

❖ I think it's going to rain.

我認為今天會下雨。

❖ Nice day, isn't it?

天氣很好，不是嗎？

重要單字

weather [ˈwɛðɚ]	天氣
forecast [ˈforkæst]	預測
umbrella [ʌmˈbrɛlə]	雨

Entertainment

娛樂

到了美國，除了觀光，上街、購物、吃喝以外，還得有娛樂，看電影、看電視、聽演唱會都是很好的娛樂，記住以下的情況英語，祝你玩得愉快。

Unit 1

Going to movies
看電影

◆ 對話一：邀約去看電影

外國人	How about going to a movie tonight? 今晚去看電影好嗎？
旅　客	Is there any good movie? 有什麼好電影？
外國人	I heard that "The Piano" is pretty good. 我聽說「鋼琴師與他的情人」很不錯。
旅　客	That sounds good. 聽起來不錯。
外國人	I'll pick you up around 6:00. 我在六點左右來接你。
旅　客	OK. I'll see you then. 好的，等一會見。

◆ 對話二：討論電影

外國人	Did you have a nice weekend? 你週末還好嗎？
旅　客	Yes. A friend and I went to the movies. 還好，我跟一個朋友去看電影。
外國人	What movie did you see? 你看了那部電影？
旅　客	"Little Women". 新小婦人。
外國人	Was it good? 好看嗎？
旅　客	Yeah. We really enjoyed it. 好看，我們都很喜歡。

◆ 對話三：看別的電影

外國人	Did you see the "Sold out" sign on the "Little Women"? 你有沒有看到「新小婦人」有個客滿的牌子？
旅　客	What? I can't believe that. 什麼？難以置信。
外國人	Well, you had better believe it! 你最好還是相信。

| 旅　客 | Let's see something else, then.
那看別的吧！ |

句型分析

→ 邀約朋友去做某某事有兩種句型：How about～?和 Would you like to～?在How about後面要加動名詞，例如：How about going to a movie?但是Would you like to後面要加原形動詞，例如：Would you like to go to a movie?

→ 去看電影，可以說go to a movie,或是go to the movies.

→ 別人提一個建議，你覺得不錯，可以回答That sounds good. sound後面加形容詞，例如good．但若說That sounds like則後面要加名詞，例如：That sounds like a good idea.

句型練習

邀約去看電影

❖ How about going to a movie tonight?
今晚去看電影好嗎？

❖ Would you like to go to a movie tonight?
今晚想去看電影嗎？

208

❖ That sounds good .

聽起來不錯。

❖ That sounds like a good idea.

聽起來是個好主意。

❖ It's been a long time since we went to the movies.

自從上次去看電影已經好久了。

 重要單字

entertainment [ɛntɚˈtenmənt]	娛樂
movie	電影
enjoy	享受
sign	牌子

旅遊錦囊

　　美國的電影院不對座位號碼,所以,遇到好看的電影,需提早去買票之外,還需提早去排隊進場,否則找不到好位子。

　　售票處,英文是box office。電影票房英文也是box office,取其售票處售出多少張票的意思。

Unit 2

Going to a Concert
去聽演唱會

◆ 對話一：去聽鄉村歌手演唱

外國人	How about going to hear a country singer tonight? 今晚去聽鄉村歌手的演唱好嗎？
旅　客	I'd enjoy that. 我喜歡去。
外國人	What's the best time to meet? 什麼時候見面最好？
旅　客	Let's say about seven. 大約七點吧。
外國人	Fine. See you then. 好的，待會兒見。

◆ 對話二：演唱會不如理想

| 外國人 | The concert was a real bomb.
這次的演唱會真是糟。 |

旅　客	I agree. 我同意。
外國人	The singing group is very popular. 這個隊很受歡迎的。
	I can't believe they would play so poorly. 我真不相信他們會演唱得這麼糟。

 句型分析

→ bomb這個字用來形容一個演出，或是電影時，表示真得很差勁，例如：The movie is a bomb.這部電影真是糟。

 句型練習

去聽演唱會

❖ Let's go to a concert.

我們去聽演唱會吧！

❖ How about going to a concert?

去聽一場演唱會，如何？

❖ Why don't we go to Michael Jackson's concert tonight?

我們今晚何不去聽麥可傑克森的演唱會？

❖ I'd enjoy that.
我很喜歡。

❖ I'd like that very much.
我非常喜歡。

❖ I'd love to.
我喜歡。

約時間

❖ How does 7:30 sound?
7點怎麼樣？

❖ Would 7:00 be O.K.?
7點好嗎？

❖ Let's say about 6:00.
我們說定6點。

重要單字

concert ['kansət]	演唱會
country	鄉村的
singer	歌手
bomb [bɑm]	很糟的演出
expect	期待
popular ['pɑpjələ˞]	受歡迎的

Unit 3

Watching Television
看電視

◆ 對話一：有什麼節目

旅　　客	What's on Channel 2 at 8:00? 8點第二台有什麼節目？
外國人	If I remember correctly, there's a quiz show. 如果我沒記錯的話，是機智問答。
旅　　客	Do you want to watch it? 你想看嗎？
外國人	Let's see what else is on first. 讓我們先看看還有什麼節目。
旅　　客	You may look in the TV Guide. 你可以看電視週刊。

◆ 對話二：有什麼節目

旅　　客	Is there anything worth watching on another channel? 其他台有沒有值得看的節目？

外國人	I think there's a western on. 我想有個西部片在演。
旅　客	Are you interested in watching it? 你有沒有興趣看？
外國人	Well, I am not sure. 嗯，我不知道。

◆ 對話三：新聞氣象

旅　客	The weather is on before the news, isn't it? 氣象在新聞之前，不是嗎？
外國人	Is it? I've got a feeling it's after the news. 是嗎？我認為氣象應該是在新聞之後。

句型分析

→ 電視頻道，英文是channel，問電視上在播放什麼節目，是What's on?問幾點幾號電視頻道上在播放什麼？是What's on channel～at幾點？

→ 問有沒有值得看的節目，值得worth後面要加動名詞，Is there anything worth watching?

→ 有沒有興趣看，be interested in後面也要加動名詞，例如：Are you interested in watching?

214

 句型練習

有什麼節目

❖ What's on Channel 8 at 8:00?

8點第八台有什麼節目？

❖ Do you remember what comes on next?

你記不記得下一個節目是什麼？

❖ Do you know what's on after the news?

你知不知道新聞之後是什麼節目？

❖ Do you mind if we watch the movie on Channel 4?

我們看4號台的電影好不好？

❖ Don't change channel. I am watching.

不要轉台，我還在看。

 重要單字

weather [ˈwɛðə]	天氣
news	新聞
channel [ˈtʃænl̩]	頻道
next	下一個
quiz show	猜謎節目
TV Guide	電視週刊
western	西部片

國家圖書館出版品預行編目資料

世界最簡單：自助旅行英語/施孝昌 著.
-- 新北市：哈福企業有限公司, 2023.03
　面；　公分. --（英語系列）；82）
ISBN　978-626-96765-9-0　（平裝）
1.CST: 英語 2.CST: 旅遊 3.CST: 會話
805.188

免費下載QR Code音檔
行動學習，即刷即聽

世界最簡單: 自助旅行英語
（附 QR Code 線上學習音檔）

作者／施孝昌
責任編輯／ Lisa Wang
封面設計／李秀英
內文排版／ 林樂娟
出版者／哈福企業有限公司
地址／新北市淡水區民族路 110 巷 38 弄 7 號
電話／ (02) 2808-4587
傳真／ (02) 2808-6545
郵政劃撥／ 31598840
戶名／哈福企業有限公司
初版／ 2023 年 3 月　七版／ 2024 年 08 月
台幣定價／ 349 元（附 QR Code 線上 MP3)
港幣定價／ 116 元（附 QR Code 線上 MP3)
封面內文圖 / 取材自 Shutterstock

全球華文國際市場總代理／采舍國際有限公司
地址／新北市中和區中山路 2 段 366 巷 10 號 3 樓
電話／ (02) 8245-8786
傳真／ (02) 8245-8718
網址／ www.silkbook.com 新絲路華文網

香港澳門總經銷／和平圖書有限公司
地址／香港柴灣嘉業街 12 號百樂門大廈 17 樓
電話／ (852) 2804-6687
傳真／ (852) 2804-6409

email ／ welike8686@Gmail.com
facebook ／ Haa-net 哈福網路商城

電子書格式：PDF